DATING *season*

Books 1 & 2

DATING *Season*

Books 1 & 2

LAURELIN PAIGE AND KAYTI MCGEE

Paige Press, LLC
Leander, Texas

Ebook ISBN: 978-1-953520-45-6

Paperback ISBN: 978-1-953520-46-3

Content Editing: Paula Dawn at Lilypad Lit

CopyEditing: Erica Russikoff at Erica Edits

Proofing: Michele Ficht, Kimberly Ruiz

Cover: Laurelin Paige

SPRING FLING

EPISODE 1

Spring is for new beginnings, and Finn's abs are a perfect introduction to dating.

Boulder is starting to thaw, seeds are being planted, and I am determined that I will sprout this season too. Starting with one particularly muscular, earnest trainer:

First I get to enjoy his rock-hard body.
Then he'll help me get one of my own.
It'll end with a different kind of rock altogether.

All I have to do is become the kind of girl who doesn't mostly just rock paint-stained pajamas.

PRAISE FOR SPRING FLING

"A delicious, sexy, clever story with fun, modern twists that feels like a night out with your best friends as they share their hilarious dating tales!"

LAUREN BLAKELY, #1NYT
BESTSELLING AUTHOR

"The best Melanie Harlow book ever written by Laurelin and Kayti. Minus the dapper black beanie. There's no such thing."

MELANIE HARLOW, USA TODAY
BESTSELLING AUTHOR AND NOTED
FASHION CRITIC

"A fun, smart, and highly addictive romance read guaranteed to give you a smile."

KYLIE SCOTT, NYT BESTSELLING AUTHOR

"This is SuperFun! I can't wait until the next installment. Chloe is hilarious, and I feel seen!"

SARINA BOWEN, USA TODAY BESTSELLING AUTHOR

"Sexy and hilarious. Dating Season is an absolute delight!"

CLAIRE CONTRERAS, NYT BESTSELLING AUTHOR

"Dating Season is a hilarious hit of rom-com goodness. I laughed, I cringed and laughed some more over the hilarious dating antics. I can't wait for more of Chloe's adventures in dating!"

HELENA HUNTING, NYT BESTSELLING AUTHOR

"Five OMG fun, bantery stars for the can't-miss romcom of the year! Buckle up for swoony slow-burn action, quirky side characters, and workout fiascos that will tickle you down to your toes."

ANNIKA MARTIN, NYT BESTSELLING AUTHOR

"Short, sweet, and funny AF! *Dating Season* is everything you love about listening to your BFF's dating drama, but better because you can actually laugh out loud without feeling like a jerk. A guilt-free guilty pleasure!"

BB EASTON, USA TODAY BESTSELLING AUTHOR

"Delightful, sexy, spunky and fun, I can't wait for more of Chloe's dating adventures. Is it too early to say #TeamAustin?"

TESSA BAILEY, NYT BESTSELLING AUTHOR

"Dating Season is a hilariously goofy, humorously insightful romp of a series from Laurelin Paige and Kayti McGee. As Chloe pines for her friend Austin but doesn't have the courage to announce her feelings, she dates her way through bad match after bad match, love dangling under her nose as the slow burn builds. I love what McGee and Paige have done and can't wait to read more! Infectious rom com fun!"

JULIA KENT, NYT BESTSELLING AUTHOR

ONE

"IS this the hill you're going to die on, Chloe?" Boy, if I had a quarter for every time someone asked me that. And then another for every time I did, in fact, die on said hill...well, I would have to drop "starving" from my artist bio.

The Instagram-worthy eyebrows of my bestie challenge me to stand behind today's bold statement —that I prefer to be alone.

My brain frantically rummages through my extensive collection of history facts, trying to find one that applies to modern times. Since women can no longer be arrested or considered a prostitute for going on a date, I'm not sure how to answer Charlotte's question in a way that makes it believable. No one *wants* to die on a hill alone, do they? Unfortunately, I may. Unlike me, most twenty-six-year-olds are proactively seeking their other half, succumbing to their biological clocks which are ticking down the tragic seconds until they die...not alone.

"What's wrong with being a lone wolf?" is all I can come up with.

"Nothing. But...humans aren't wired to be alone. We're pack animals by nature." Narrowed brown eyes pin me to the sofa. "Plus, I know why you're choosing to not date anyone, so it's my duty, as your best friend, to give you a nudge in the right direction." With a whirl of her chair, she turns back to the computer she's convinced holds my future partner.

I drain my second glass of Merlot and slump into the leather of Charlotte's couch, silently asking it to swallow me whole so I won't have to go through with her outlandish idea of finding me a man via dating app. When I arrived at Charlotte's place, I had no idea this was an intervention of sorts. This visit was supposed to be chilling with wine and flower shopping for Charlotte's upcoming wedding. Instead, I've been bamboozled with an online matchmaking site that will have men sending a rock, if they're interested in me. Not the kind on Charlotte's finger, a poorly drawn stone rock to symbolize the building of a solid foundation.

How can I take this seriously when I'm not impressed with their branding?

"Granny Mae would not approve of this," I counter, since history has failed to provide me with an adequate defense. "You know how she feels about the internet." Maybe I'm not playing fair using Charlotte's adoration of my grandmother and her questionable southern charm, but desperate times call for desperate measures, so I continue, *"Full of damn trolls* I believe were her exact words."

Charlotte gasps at my underhanded attempt to thwart her plan, but is undeterred. "Granny Mae is in North Carolina. Probably making biscuits, with her sweet little granny hands. Besides, she'll never have to know how you met the love of your life. You'll blow her bonnet off when you go home to visit." She points to the website with smiling people on the screen. "Look, it's called FriendsOfFriends, so that's respectable. F-O-F. And you know what that O is for!"

"Of?"

Charlotte glances over her shoulder at me. "Wow, this is why you never get laid."

Never is a bit harsh. It's not like I've intentionally chosen to be celibate for years. Well, maybe I have, but there's no time to respond with more grannyisms about the dangers of social media, because the front door opens and in walks the reason for my nun-like state and Charlotte's insistence that I give this a try.

"What's up, ladies?" Austin, Charlotte's roommate extraordinaire, drawls in his husky timbre that warms my wine and brings the fine hairs on the nape of my neck to attention.

"Hey," I say, sitting a bit straighter. "How was work?"

"Busy." He deposits a white to-go box on the counter separating the kitchen and living room. "What do you have for me today, Chloe?"

For a moment, I can't think. He truly is extraordinary, in an understated way. Dark eyes, dark hair, and a dark sense of humor. He's the holy trinity in my book. But, like all good things, he's taken. So I can only mope and admire his tall frame from atop my lonely dying-hill.

"Forks were once thought to be sacrilegious," I finally say.

He chuckles and leans against the counter, crossing his arms. "Why is that?"

"When they were introduced in the 11th century, they were considered artificial hands and as such, an offense to God."

"Amazing. You never disappoint me, Chloe." And his amusement at my gems of worthless knowledge never disappoints *me*. "I've got something for you, too. A customer ordered fettuccine Alfredo, and while I was making it, they canceled due to carb-guilt." He winks at me. "I know you love to eat, so I brought it home for you."

Three concerns immediately present themselves.

1. The fact that he expected me to be here is troublesome. For someone who wants to be alone, I'm always hanging out here to avoid being alone. Maybe I do need a date.

2. Austin is a phenomenal chef, so although I hate being predictable, I'll take the fettuccine. Seems fair. He feeds me delicious pasta, and I feed him useless history facts.

3. He cannot see what we are doing. Sure, he's got a girlfriend, but do I want him to think I'm off the table? Not that I'm on the table. But I might be? Some day?

"Thank you. That was really thoughtful." Faster than Austin can dice an onion, I spring from the couch and cross to Charlotte's desk, positioning myself to block the screen.

He ambles closer, bringing the seductive scent of garlic with him. "What are you—"

"It's lady underwear stuff," I half shout, at the same time Charlotte says, "Setting up a dating app."

Austin's eyes volley between us.

"A dating app...for Charlotte," I amend. This is not my finest cover-up.

He stops a few feet from my raised hand and gives me side-eye. "Charlotte's engaged."

"She may need a fling." I shrug. "Don't shame her sexual needs."

"I do need to know I'm still desirable," Charlotte adds, because besties roll with stuff like this. "I'm a modern gal in a post-modern world, bud."

He grazes his bottom lip with a peek of white teeth, and then, like the laid-back guy he is, lets it go. "Okay. Keep your secrets. I'm going to shower and nap before I meet Lucy."

Right. Lucy. The totally put-together new girlfriend with a successful career in public relations.

"Let me know how you like the fettuccine," he calls on his way out of the room.

When he's disappeared down the hallway, Charlotte whispers, "You know, you're doing this to get over him. So it's okay if he knows. Because...you're moving on?"

"Shhhh. He doesn't know about my crush. And never will. Because you would never, ever tell him, upon pain of death. Right?"

"I'm offended. Girl Code is more sacred than the cross."

"You're Jewish."

"It's the principle."

"Well, I'm already nervous enough about going out with strangers, I don't need him making me *more* nervous. He'll have me convinced they're all serial killers."

Actually, I don't really need convincing on that part. Granny Mae convinced me years ago.

"They're hardly strangers," Charlotte reassures. "They're friends of friends on your social media. Who are going to give you an O—"

"Stop, please," I cut her off. "I need to eat my feelings with cream sauce. Want some?"

"I do, but no. I have a fitting for my wedding dress soon."

See, Charlotte doesn't understand what it's like to put yourself on the internet. She's been with her man since high school. If only my high school boyfriend hadn't been a jerk, I could be in Charlotte's position. Thanks for nothing, Josh. Ten minutes later, when I've settled into a chair next to Charlotte with warmed pasta—and more wine— Austin reappears. "How is it?"

"Delicious, as usual." Even if it's now stuck in my throat at the sight of his damp, rumpled hair.

"Good. I'm heading over to Lucy's now, because she wants to nap with me."

A nap date. Could life be more unfair? I love naps.

Austin's crooked grin before he leaves is beguiling, and really, it's best I do this dating thing because no one should be so enamored with the smile of such a good friend of theirs.

"Why can't all men be like Austin?" I murmur, twirling fettuccine in an endless spiral on my fork.

"They can be, Chloe." Charlotte places a hand on my knee. "You're so focused on the tree, you can't see the forest. It's time to say *timber*."

Maybe it's the alcohol lowering my defenses, but she's right. Austin *is* one of my favorite people. He brings me unexpected meals and laughs at my history trivia, but that's as far as it goes. "Let's do this, before I change my mind."

She smiles. "While you were focused on Austin's...noodle," I choke briefly, "I set up the account with your email. Your password is forkme." Charlotte's pink nails fly across the keyboard and navigate to the profile page. "First, we need a cute picture to entice the forest. Got any selfies?"

"No. I'm not a selfie taker. I'm a meme saver."

She lifts her phone and aims it at me. "Smile."

This is happening too fast. Although I'm only half invested, I'd like to at least look like I didn't crawl out of a hole. She gives me a few minutes to release my hair from its messy bun, remove a stray peppercorn from my incisor, and apply a bit of lip gloss. After a few awkward poses, trying to get that "oh, you caught me off guard" natural look down, my face smiles back at me on the monitor.

In the age of Photoshop and Facetune, I hope I win points for my non-filtered photo. I've never considered myself vain, but it's impossible not to critique myself and find every flaw. How many strangers will see this image and based on it, decide whether they'd have sex with me? FriendsOfFriends needs a disclaimer box where I can explain that I hibernate in the winter, but now that it's spring, I shaved my legs and made an appointment for fresh highlights.

"Should we take another?" I ask. Perhaps one Charlotte poses for.

"No. It's perfect. You look like the girl next door." She gives me the reassuring statistic that women who post a photo are twice as likely to get a response and tabs to the next section. "Job."

I retrieve the wine and pour us each a generous serving. "Can we put what I'm supposed to be doing?"

"There's nothing wrong with being a potter. Not everyone is qualified to make pottery."

"Yes, this is true." But I'm supposed to be a

director at an art museum, selling my own art on the side. And calling "teaching children how to make wobbly cups at *It's Clay Time*" being a potter is overly kind. That unfulfilled dream is the entire reason I picked Boulder for college and am still here in Colorado. Oh, well. Van Gogh sold one painting during his lifetime, so there's still hope for me if I do croak on my hill. Being a pottery teacher may not be my dream, but neither is this dating site. As we've established, we can't always get what we want. "Okay, next."

"What's Your Idea of a Perfect Date?" Charlotte laughs. "Didn't you once say the perfect date was going to Nathan's Hot-Dog Eating Contest?"

"That was before I knew nap dates existed. Plus, I was hungry when I said it. And anyway, you *still* think a Tool concert is a good place to meet guys."

We continue on, filling in details, and this is all so self-esteem draining. There's a whole "Get To Know Me" section and what if no one is charmed by my fascination with tiny houses and passion for art? And on the flip side, what if I'm not charmed by any of them? Despite the churning in my belly, we continue on, until the profile is complete.

Charlotte looks over at me with her finger hovering on the enter key. "You ready to publish?"

"No." Right now, my hill doesn't seem so bad.

"Granny Mae would say it's spring, the perfect time to plant some seeds and see what grows."

"She'd also be planting those seeds to annoy her neighbor. Granny Mae is no angel."

"And that's why I love her."

With a gleam in her eyes, Charlotte clicks submit.

TWO

A WISE ART teacher once told me—if something isn't inspiring you, find one detail to focus on and build from there. That's what I'm now doing with Peter, one of twenty potential matches FriendsOf-Friends has picked for me.

This site takes matchmaking seriously, y'all. Within thirty minutes of Charlotte creating my profile, the rocks started pummeling me. Now I have to sift through the rubble, and find someone that's interesting.

Peter's rugged face smiles at me from the computer screen, and I hone in on the dapper black beanie on his head.

"If you squint your eyes, he kind of looks like Austin in that hat." I clink my wine glass against the beer he's holding. "Cheers, Peter."

"Stop." Charlotte's laugh tinkles in the room for a very long time, it seems. She's a chronic giggler when she's drinking, whereas I'm a melancholy mopey-head. Charlotte's words, not mine. "You're getting *over* him, so you can't only date guys that remind you of him."

"It's *my* rebound."

"...no it's not."

I choose to ignore her and instead highlight Peter's interests with the mouse. "He likes cheese and ice-fishing. Does that go together?"

"Who cares? You love cheese."

Fair enough. The beanie earns Peter a tentative rock. This site needs a variety of rocks to offer, corresponding to the level of interest. Pebble, stone, boulder. Marketing had one job. On a sigh, I swipe to the next guy. Hunter is an attractive accountant who enjoys cruising the open road on his motorcycle.

Charlotte loves him.

"Ooh, I bet he's covered in tattoos under that button-down shirt." She bumps her shoulder to mine. "Doesn't the artist in you want to find out?"

"What if it's something stupid, like...money? And then I have to pretend to love it?"

"You can draw something exciting for his next one."

I'm not sure it's fair to put that kind of pressure

on poor Hunter. There's no way he can compete with the *Stairway to Heaven* music notes ascending up Austin's arm. However, I could get free tax help *and* he has dark eyes. The scales are tilting in Hunter's favor, much like the room after all this wine. His bio says he's spent so much time with his friends he's forgotten how to meet people. I can relate.

"Okay, let's give him a rock."

We muddle through the next prospects, and they're disappointing. Not one listed nap-dates in their interests. Now that I know that exists, I'm obsessed. I'm a champion napper. I'm sure Austin and Lucy are snuggled in a perfect spoon right now while he plays with her split-end-free hair.

"That guy mows my mom's yard," Charlotte exclaims, when I swipe to a beefy man with a bald head. "He's so polite. And reliable."

I shake my head. "No way. No rock for Yard Guy."

"Why?"

"It's too close to home. Think about it. If it didn't work out, your mom's yard would be the victim and she'd never forgive me. I adore your mom and don't want to lose her."

She agrees and we move on. The next candidate

is another person that's too close to home. But this time, I don't mind.

"Nope," Charlotte says. "Eli works with Austin."

Exactly. I'd see Austin all the time. "Is that so bad?"

"Bad. Very bad. Let's exclude some friends so you're not tempted."

We make adjustments in settings to eliminate certain mutuals and resume the process. An older man with chestnut hair and light-brown eyes captures my attention. He's into biographies and camping.

"Oh my God. Matthew is a sleep doctor. I bet he's great at napping."

Charlotte tsks and points her wine glass at me. "I need to address something. Your three picks all have something you associate with Austin."

Silent, I slip Matthew a rock, and slide to the next person.

"I saw that."

"And? I'm trying to build upon what I like."

"Yes, you're building a monument to Austin." She commandeers the mouse. "Let's find some variety. You need a buffet, Chloe. Load your plate with things besides basic chicken."

I laugh. "Did you just call Austin basic?" He's

anything but basic. "In the poultry world, he's Granny Mae's famous fried chicken." And I'll never get to taste him. Now, I've sunk deeper into the melancholy phase. "I should give up and move home."

"What? No way."

"Nothing is going according to plan."

"Sometimes you have to make a new plan."

If only it were that easy. I didn't *plan* to fall for a friend who doesn't feel the same.

"Be right back," I say.

I scoot away from the desk and bolt toward the bathroom, so Charlotte can't see the stupid tears welling in my eyes. The hallway teeter-totters as I sway on what have morphed into Jell-O legs. I swing open the door, rest my back against the wood, and close my eyes. I'm not sure why this is freaking me out so much. It *would* be nice to have someone be my better half. The hand-holding. The inside jokes. Couple stuff.

It's just that I always pictured that someone as Austin.

Kurt Vonnegut said, "History is merely a list of surprises. It can only prepare us to be surprised yet again." Well, imagine my surprise to see I am not in the bathroom when I open my eyes. I'm in Austin's room. I've never actually been in here before. It always seemed too personal.

His guitar rests in the corner, and on his organized bookshelf is the gift I made him for Christmas. A pottery dish to hold his picks. I try not to squee aloud. His fawn-colored walls are decorated with abstract art, but what's really grabbed my attention is the headboard of his king-sized bed. It's a masculine dark oak with a cutout below the curve of wood. And hanging from that cutout...are steel handcuffs.

In my inebriated state, am I seeing things? I blink a few times. I am not.

I tiptoe closer, and yep, it's handcuffs.

He's a chef, not a police officer. So unless he's trying to fix a sleep-walking problem, Austin is kinky. I can't even with this information. Am I into that? My body's reaction says I am. It's hot. And now I'm hot. And trespassing. Maybe he'll arrest me. Okay, I need to get out of here.

I inch open the door, peek out, and dart across the hall to where I should've been all along. After splashing cool water on my now-red face, I return to the living room.

Charlotte is where I left her, typing away on the keyboard. "I've decided, we gotta do the exact opposite of Austin," she says.

"Terrible and boring?"

"This is why you're single. No, I mean, doesn't play guitar at parties in his beanie. Isn't a chef."

Doesn't handcuff you to the bed. "Like, your guy listens to hip-hop and works in an office."

"Sounds terrible and boring to me."

"Well, I've messaged a half dozen who fit the description already, while you were in the bathroom." She stands. "Let's put the app on your phone and find more food."

For whatever reason, while we forage the refrigerator, I don't disclose my discovery in Austin's bedroom. Once the app is downloaded, it's decided I'm staying the night so we can continue our efforts. We settle on the couch and keep swiping through candidates until there's no one left.

"Now, we wait," Charlotte says. "First guy that messages back is the one you'll go out with, no matter what."

"Okay."

"It's like the universe decides that way. Right?" She holds up her pinkie. "Pinkie swear."

On the third try, my finger loops around hers, and I agree.

DRINKING TOO many glasses of wine means you have to deal with your horrible choices the next morning. Hazy memories of pinkies and handcuffs cloud my pounding head as I untangle myself from the blanket swaddling me on the coach. I sit up and rub my temples to ease the ache. My phone makes an annoying vibration against the coffee table every few minutes.

A notification from FriendsOfFriends informs me I have ten messages waiting. My curiosity leads me to the app. No matter what's there, or how horrified I am at my drunken choices, I know you can't break a pinkie swear. Please, let the universe have been kind.

Lucky for me, the first message in my inbox is not terrible. Or boring.

"Oh," I murmur when I see the dark-haired, blue-eyed man smiling in the little circle.

His name is Finn, and I don't even remember giving him a rock. Before I read his message, I look him up to refresh my memory and dang, but the Drunk C's have amazing taste in hot bodies.

"Hi," his simple message reads.

Okay. Short and sweet. It's charming.

I take a deep breath and write back "Hey! Nice to meet you!" but immediately erase it. The exclamation points make me seem too excited.

I try again. "What's up?"

Ugh. I erase that too. What if he says his dick? He may be ungodly attractive, but that doesn't mean he's not a pervert. Granny Mae has forwarded me a few articles about the scourge of internet peen pics.

After overanalyzing and erasing a few more responses, I finally type back, "Hi."

While I wait for a response, I scroll through the remaining messages, but no one gives me that wow feeling like Finn. The other guys have all written paragraphs that give me immediate red flags. As I'm thanking the universe for my good fortune with Finn, the other aspect of this app hits me like a ton of—pardon the pun—rocks.

Rejection.

Someone is always going to be the loser in the game of love. That's sad to realize. What's the etiquette here? Do I ignore these other guys, and they'll think I'm busy? They're strangers, yes, but they're also people with feelings. It seems harsh to leave them hanging.

I'm nothing if not polite, even if they're damn trolls, so I go through each one and reply with—

"Thank you for your interest. You're awesome, but unfortunately, I'm not a good match for you. I hope you find someone that rocks your world!"

There. Do unto others and all that.

A message pops up. From Finn.

"That's too bad. You intrigued me with the tiny houses."

Wait. What? *Of course* I also sent that rejection message to Finn, because life can never be easy.

"I'm so sorry! I didn't mean to send that to you. It was intended for someone else."

"Ah, letting them down easy. I feel bad for the guy missing out on you. Glad it's not me."

Oh my. A foreign rush of warmth works its way through my system. Can you blush on the inside? I remember last night's discovery. Yes, you definitely can. Only this one is far more appropriate.

Unsure what to say back to that gem, I type out, "That's definitely going to get you in my panties," but then erase, for obvious reasons. I send a safe smiling emoji with "Me too."

"So, how does this work?" he asks. "Do we text first? Then ease into a meeting?"

"Your guess is as good as mine. This is my first time using a dating app."

"Well, let's do it. I know it's soon, but I'm not the kind of guy to wait around. Life is short. So...are you free tomorrow? Breakfast? Lunch? Dinner?"

Well, I wasn't expecting a date to happen right away. I envisioned a long courtship via text would take place. Something vaguely old-fashioned to ease me in. But best not to drag it out, I guess. What if I fall in love with his words and it's all a sham? People are much different face-to-face. Maybe he has a laugh that frightens birds off light poles. Or a habit of speaking to my chin. We could have zero chemistry. Time to rip the Band-Aid off and see what happens.

"I'm teaching a pottery class in the morning. But I'm free after five."

"Cool. How about seven? You can choose the place."

We talk a few more minutes, and so far, this isn't painful. He's nice. No warning sirens are blaring from his replies. And he's not afraid to use the app emojis. It's cute. He promises to message me later, and when I collect my things to tiptoe past a snoring Charlotte, I'm grinning like a loon.

THREE

THE INTERNET IS both a blessing and a curse. A blessing because you have endless information at your fingertips. Anything and everything is just a few clickety-clacks away. And a curse, well...because you have endless information at your fingertips. Anything and everything is a few clickety-clacks away.

Like dating tips.

This morning, rabbit-holing before my class arrived, I stumbled upon an article that said choosing an exciting place for a first date increases the chance of the other person falling for you. Craft fairs are probably only thrilling to me, so I've got about four hours to pick a place. But how exciting do I want to be? What if he falls for me and I don't reciprocate?

"How's this?" Louis, a carrot-topped six-year-old

asks, saving me from the Pandora's box of anxieties I've opened in my mind, and preserving my hope.

I praise his misshapen bowl. "It's beautiful."

"Grown-ups are bad liars."

Kids are sometimes hard to deal with in my weekend pottery class. The tiny humans are amazingly intuitive.

"Well first of all, that really depends on the grown-up. But second of all, I'm not." I am. "Everyone sees something different in art, Louis."

"What do you see?" he asks.

"I see something with character, that your mom will treasure. Something you put a lot of effort into designing." I run my finger around the thumb-sized dent in the side. "It has a belly button. It's one of a kind."

He beams, while next to him, Gwen, a ten-year-old artist in the making, frowns at her perfect round bowl.

I lean in and whisper, "Yours is exquisite."

"It looks like every other bowl. There's nothing special about it."

"Of course there is. You created it by hand. That's special." I finish lying badly and untie my apron. "Okay, listen, everyone. This class is about having fun. You can't go wrong. Don't put so much pressure on yourself." You've got your whole adulthood to do that. "Let's place them on the shelf to dry, and tomorrow, we'll paint them."

A frenzy of chatter and energy erupts in the large classroom filled with pottery wheels. Six little bodies bounce behind me to the wall lined with cubbies where they place their creations. Finn is temporarily forgotten in a rush of washing hands and parent pickup.

By the time I've cleaned up the room and headed out for my lunch break, the Hill is already bustling with people out and about in the warm sunshine.

I stroll down the block to my favorite cafe and find an available patio table to enjoy my burger while I clickety-clack the internet for exciting date ideas. Gwen's innocent statement about her bowl lingers in my mind. There's always plenty to do in Boulder—shopping, museums, dining—but everything seems so not special. I'm sure Finn has explored every valley and peak surrounding the Flatirons. There's a ton of breweries to tour, but again, that reeks of ordinary.

My grandmother always says, "Don't look for a man who makes you feel special. Any man can do that. Find a man who believes you are, and he'll do things for you he's never done for anyone else." Well, I guess that goes both ways. And now the pressure to find a place that stands out increases twofold.

"How's your day going?" pops up on my phone from Finn.

"Good! On my lunch break. How's yours going?"

Bonus points for Finn. He doesn't tell me, he shows me. A photo comes through, and oh my, Finn at the gym is lethal. In a snug black T-shirt and gray gym shorts, he gives me a charming grin that's framed by scruff along his masculine jaw. Behind him is a mirrored wall and I zoom all the way in to enjoy the reflected rear view. This is not a man who skips leg day. Or ass day. If that is a day. I've not seen the inside of a gym in...well, ever. I'm by no means a couch potato, but I also didn't leave the mayo off my cheeseburger. Or my fries.

"Impressive," I type back. "While you're busy working out, I'm busy working on this."

On impulse, I snap a photo of my food and send it.

"Mmm...you're making me hungry."

His three m's cause me to shift in my chair. Maybe I *do* need to get laid.

"Have you picked the place yet?"

"Working on it. I've narrowed down my choices and will let you know soon."

He clearly can't tell I am a bad-liar-grown-up through text, finishing the conversation with an adorable smiling emoji. Part of me wishes I'd let him plan the date. The pressure to find somewhere out of the ordinary very nearly ruins my appetite for more mayonnaise. Until a man, wearing a Colorado Avalanche hat, sits at the table across from me. Ah-ha! Hockey. I'm trying to do things I wouldn't normally, and Finn is obviously an active person.

It's perfect. Thank you, stranger.

My appetite is saved.

TO SAY I'm on the verge of hyperventilating is an understatement. I hate that stranger. What's better than being a spectator, I had thought. Being *on* the ice, I had thought. I'd had the brilliant idea that we'd learn to play a game of hockey. With nothing but our first names and an email address I'll likely get coupons on for the next decade, I was able to secure our spots for Stick and Puck at Sport Zone.

It's just that in all my excitement, I'd sort of forgotten I haven't ice-skated since eighth grade.

So as I stand outside waiting for Finn to arrive, I'm resisting the urge to cancel. I'm going to make a fool out of myself in front of someone I want to like me. For the first time, my brain is percolating with dating tips instead of history facts. The internet article I found said a study came to the conclusion people determine attraction within three seconds of meeting. That's astounding. How can you decide that in such a short amount of time? People become more attractive as you get to know them. There are nuances to personality that contribute to attraction and—

Forget all that, apparently the study is true. I am definitely attracted to the tall, lean body dressed in jeans and a black button-down shirt striding toward me at a brisk clip.

"Chloe?" he asks as he approaches.

His voice is smooth and rich enough to make my bones putty.

I smile and internally squee. "Yep. Finn?"

His broad shoulders relax. "Thank God you didn't catfish me."

"Catfish *you*?"

He's the one who looked like a magazine fitness model. But pictures did not do this man justice. Blue eyes peer at me from behind black frames and I may have just discovered a Clark Kent fetish.

He smirks. "You could've been scamming me. People do crazy things. I know someone who met a girl who had a whole stock photo family."

"Really? Well, I guess that gives a whole new meaning to a picture-perfect family."

While his eyes do a sweep of my body, I can't

help but wonder if I passed the three-second test. Since the date is casual, I opted for my favorite skinny jeans, a French-tucked plaid shirt, and heeled boots. Charlotte approved but said to "show the man some titty," because she is a classy bride-to-be. So at the last minute, I slipped open a few buttons to reveal a provocative glimpse of cleavage.

Her suggestion worked, because his glance lingers on my breasts just a tad longer than appropriate. Sweet. I passed. God, he probably has abs under that shirt that's clinging to him. If this date goes well, I might get to lick them at some point. Very exciting prospect.

"No scamming here. You're not a serial killer, are you?"

He laughs and it, too, is perfect—low and husky. "No."

"Phew. Then again, I'm sure they all say that."

"If you'd feel safer, I can text my driver's license to one of your friends?"

Maybe he's joking, but it actually would make me feel better. "Would you mind?" Okay, I know that probably kills the mood. But better the mood than me, right? I may have inherited Granny Mae's penchant for one-liners after all.

He reaches in his pocket and removes a silver clip holding some money and a few cards. Within a minute, Charlotte now knows who to come looking for if anything happens.

"Thank you, Finn," I say. "This is all kind of strange, huh?"

"Stranger things have happened, I'm sure." He gives a sexy head nod toward the sprawling building behind me. "So, what are we doing?"

His brows rise as I explain what tonight will entail.

"Wow. Very cool."

Another study showed that remembering snippets about a person is not only flattering but also shows interest. I give it a go and hope I don't sound like a stalker.

"I gathered you were athletic from your profile, and you said you like winter, so I thought this would be fun."

These date-studiers are onto something. His gaze locks with mine with what can only be interpreted as awe. "I'm impressed."

"Ready?"

"Are you?" he challenges in a way that makes me feel as if he's not really talking about the ice. Which, of course, I'm not either way.

His hand lands on the small of my back and as he leads me inside, dating factoids pop like popcorn in my head.

Say his name to show I'm attentive and connected. Done.

Blush if he pays me a compliment. Not sure how to do that on command, but I'll try.

He opens the door for me, and we cross the marble floor to the brunette at the counter that spans the back wall of glass. Behind her is a view of the rink, full of people whirling about like Olympians. Finn refuses to let me pay—aw—and we walk away with basic instructions and coupons to the onsite dining area. Once skated up, my worst fears are realized the moment my ass hits the cold hard ice. An "oomph" barrels out of me.

"Oh, shit," Finn says, before bending down to help me stand from my sprawled position. "You okay?"

"I'm fine." If I'm not, I'm unaware because our bodies are now melded. I grip his hips for balance and his woodsy scent is amazing.

His brow furrows. "Can you handle a stick?"

I nod. So many pucking puns crawl up my tongue, but I keep them trapped inside my mouth.

"You sure?" His hands caress my shoulders. "We can go sit down."

"I'm sure. My butt will recover."

"Good to hear. It's a very nice butt." He winks.

And there it is. The blush. Blush is a demure

word for what's happening to my face. It feels as though I stuck my head in a five hundred degree kiln. Our instructor arrives and the moment is lost but not forgotten. It's all I can think about as we volley the puck back and forth. Finn whizzes across the ice like a professional player, and by the time we finish our session, my thighs are screaming.

In the rink's restaurant, we segue to the getting-to-know-you part of our date. On a scale of one to awkward, I'd give it a solid seven. Three points have been deducted because Finn was not captivated by the Hip Check sampler I ordered and there is just no ladylike way to eat buffalo wings or loaded nachos. Particularly as your date enjoys a grilled chicken salad. He tells me about his job as a personal trainer at a SuperFit gym and listens with rapt attention as I give him the lowdown on my Van Gogh pottery dreams.

"So," Finn says, when we're outside the arena, standing beside my car, "what now?"

His tongue shines his lips like gloss and as much as I'd like to disrobe in this parking lot, that darn dating tip article recommends against it. Sex before three dates gives a man the wrong idea.

"I have to wake early in the morning," I say. "Pottery class. I should get going."

He moves in closer. "I'd like to see you again."

"I'd like that too."

After we exchange phone numbers, he tilts my chin up and here it comes. He's going to kiss me. I'm so ready for this, I close my eyes. Hold my breath. And then—

Our first kiss happens.

A gentlemanly brush of his lips on my forehead.

Huh. Don't get me wrong, my forehead is feeling all kinds of things, but my lips are confused and jealous.

He opens my door and promises to call. Even if there was no lip action, as I drive away, I'd say it was a good date. Complete with butterflies and blushes. He's swoony and cute, and most important, I only thought about Austin once.

FOUR

I THINK TOO MUCH. It's exhausting. Usually, I'm consumed with non-stressful thoughts of my next clay creation or diving down yet another rabbit hole of how things originated in history. But there's been a breach. Ever since last night, I've analyzed every nook and cranny of why Finn didn't kiss me on the lips.

Perhaps I had buffalo breath.

Something in my teeth. It happens to me more than I think it happens to other people.

If I consult my history books, there's a slim chance the smooch didn't happen because I never got around to exposing a wrist or ankle to confirm my interest in him and pique his in me.

It could be anything. Or it could be nothing. Whatever the reason, it's messing with my mojo.

"Does my dinosaur look like a dog?" Louis asks.

I tilt my head and debate how to answer, ideally truthfully. "Well, dogs aren't green, so no."

He smiles and continues dolloping paint on his bowl.

As I check on the other painters, Andrea, my co-worker, enters the room with a Cheshire Cat grin on her face. "Chloe, someone is here to see you. I'll take over."

She doesn't respond to my quizzical eyebrow raise, so I let the class know I'll be back soon. I trod to the front of the store where a few customers sift through clearance items. Behind them, I spot my visitor, shrouded in a ray of sunshine, by the art supplies.

"Hey, babe," Finn says.

"Hi..." My body doesn't know how to react to his unexpected visit. The way he said "babe" did things to me in a heart-thumping way, but I'm also not good with surprises. It's like having one nipple hard, and one not.

"You look cute," he says, when I close the distance between us.

I beam at his compliment, even if it's generous. My hair is in a rough-shod bun and the paint-smeared apron over my leggings and tunic top is not what I would've chosen had I known he was going to show up here today. He, on the other hand, looks exquisite in dark jeans and a blue polo.

"Thank you." I toy with the string wrapped around my waist as we smile at each other. "So...what are you doing here?"

"I want to take you to dinner."

"Oh. Today?"

"Yeah." He picks up a paintbrush from the shelf and fans it back and forth across his palm. "What time do you get off?"

His question sounds sexual but maybe I'm projecting. "I don't get off until four."

"Perfect. Text me your address." He tucks a wayward strand of hair behind my ear, grazing the shell. "I'll pick you up at seven?"

"That sounds good."

He holds out the brush. "I'll take this."

"You paint?"

"No."

I tilt my head and roll my lips inward. That's odd, but I guess I'll let it go? Are we to the nosy stage where I can question his purchases? I ring up his fan brush and let him know it's an excellent choice, soft and makes smooth strokes, hoping he'll say what it's for. He doesn't.

"I'll let you get back to work." He leans down to

whisper in my ear, "I find this whole artist gig sexy." And with that, he exits.

There's no time to ponder why he didn't kiss me if he finds my job sexy. Or why he buys random paintbrushes when he doesn't paint.

The next few hours are spent not lying to my class, and then I drive home to my cottage and spend two hours getting ready. Normally, I'm not high-maintenance, but I need to make up for the way I looked at the store. Plus, I was due for some lady-landscaping. Not that I'm planning on sex, but...just in case he decides to surprise me again.

Since I'm silky smooth and lotioned up, I'm going all in with a dress tonight. The long-sleeved floral dress hits mid-thigh, exposing a lot of leg.

I text a pic to Charlotte. "Which shoes?"

"You look hot! The strappy heel on your left foot."

"You sure? You don't like the boot on the right foot?"

"I'm sure!"

I kick off the boot and slip on the other heel as the doorbell rings.

"He's here! I'll let you know how it goes."

When I open the door, it's not Finn, it's June, my landlord. She isn't quite as funny or as huggable or as prone to sugar-coating as Granny Mae, but she's basically been my stand-in for the last few years.

"Hi, Chloe." She gives me a once-over. "Are you going out?" One of the disadvantages of living on June's property is there's this unspoken thing happening where she kind of keeps tabs on me.

"Yes, I have a date."

Her thin brows rise nearly to her salt and pepper hair. "Oh, well, I don't want to ruin your date."

"No, it's okay. What's up?"

"Well, I'm selling the house and moving to Florida to be near my daughter."

I blink and step onto the porch. "That's great...and unexpected."

"Don't worry, dear. If it sells fast, whoever buys it will give you thirty days to move out. I'll make sure it's in writing."

I want to throw myself at her orthopedic shoes and beg her to stay here in Colorado. But I know from our numerous tea parties over the years I've lived here, she misses her daughter the same way I miss Granny. My unselfish side wins.

"No worries. I'll start looking for something else."

"Okay, dear. Have fun on your date." She pats my arm. "Make sure you stop by for tea and give me the details."

"Will do."

She waddles across the lawn back to her house, and I drop down onto the porch swing. The universe is punishing me for thinking I lived in a tiny house. Like, "You think that's small? Well, let's see how you like this cardboard box."

Not only is this place ideal because it has a back porch where I can make my pottery, it's cheaper than most apartments. Plus, I love June. I'm in the middle of apologizing to my cottage for the slight when the purr of an engine interrupts me.

Finn.

His sleek black SUV parks next to my Honda.

"Hey," I call out.

"Wow," he says, climbing the steps, "you get better every time I see you."

The words leave my mouth before I can stop them, "Same, SuperFit, same."

He chuckles and leans against the railing. "This is a nice place. It suits you."

Don't remind me. "Yeah, I love it here."

"Ready?" he asks.

Is it bad I don't offer him a tour? It seems too soon. It's trivial, but Austin is the only man who has been inside my home. Maybe I should invite Finn in, just to show I'm moving on from my crush.

"Be right back," I say.

He waits on the porch while I grab my handbag

and keys, and I can only hope this date makes up for the bombshell June dropped on me.

SO FAR, so good. Even though it's a little weird. I'm all for buffets, especially ones with a dessert bar, but is it normal to eat nine plates? I'm in no way judging Finn's voracious appetite, but where does he keep it all? Does he have an extra stomach?

"Wow, you're still going." I've been done for forty minutes, and he's got yet another mountain of lean meats and greens.

"Bulking up, babe. We've got a competition at SuperFit I'm gonna win."

I'm guessing "babe" is the chosen pet name. As far as nicknames go, I've never had a man use one. It's got an alpha vibe, and... I'm into it. A lot. I don't know myself at all, it turns out. My personal history hadn't prepared me for the surprises to come.

He details the competition, and it sounds a bit like torture, honestly.

"What does the winner get?"

"A trophy."

"Oh, wow. I'd want cash for all that work."

"I've got plenty of cash." Must be nice. He places

the hand not eating on my knee. "You should come see me compete."

This is good. He's making future plans, and we haven't even kissed. "Okay, I'll go to your competition, and you can come to my spring thing."

"What spring thing?"

While I explain to him the upcoming craft fair, he shovels in the rest of his food.

"Sounds interesting."

I'm not sure if he means that, and it's not a commitment, but I get it. Craft fairs aren't for everyone. Austin is a trooper and goes along with me and Charlotte, but maybe it's for the kettle corn. It's divine. Austin always sneaks and buys a jumbo bag for me to take home.

I have to know, "Do you like kettle corn?"

"It's a little too sweet for me. I prefer plain."

"Plain as in no butter?"

"Yeah." He finally finishes his meal and leans in. "Is the popcorn a deal breaker?"

I laugh, but maybe. "You like what you like."

"Do you like me more than kettle corn?"

What kind of question is this? "Are you asking me to give up kettle corn?"

He chuckles. "No, but I think I could satisfy you more than kettle corn."

Finn has thrown down the gauntlet and I don't

know what to say back. I let the blush speak for itself, as recommended. Plus, the waitress arrives to refill our lemon water. By the time she leaves, it's much too late to go back to his comment with something flirtatious.

On the ride home, we discuss music, and he plays his favorite songs. I never would've pegged him for classical. Mozart and Beethoven fill the cabin and whoa, I'm turned on as his fingers dance across an imaginary piano.

As far as the seat belt will allow, I lean toward him, chin in hand on the armrest. "Do you play piano?"

"A little."

Well, that's enough for me. The soft light of the moon shades him in artistic shadows, and I could almost see a vision of me preferring him over kettle corn.

He pulls into my driveway and parks.

"So, you think you'll come see me compete?"

"I don't know. What's in it for me?" He opens and closes his mouth a couple times, and I realize he doesn't know I'm flirting. "Like...do I get to see your abs?"

"Oh." Without breaking eye contact, he lifts his shirt in a slow tease, and holy wow, he is *ripped*. I've never seen this in real life. I tentatively touch the etches on his stomach. They feel...huh. So weird. Like iron encased in velvet.

"You could have your own, you know."

His raspy voice tears my gaze from his stomach. "Oh, I don't think..."

"I could be your trainer." He grazes his teeth along his lower lip, and maybe this fitness talk is foreplay.

"Oh, yeah? You'd...spot me?" I know very few workout innuendos.

"I'd spot you a mile away."

With a groan, his hand grasps my neck, pulling me closer. And then I get my kiss. Our tongues collide and somehow I'm straddling his lap. His massive hard-on rocks into me.

"Fuck, Chloe. I want to rip your dress off right now."

I want that too. Especially when he squeezes my nipple through the thin material.

"Mm. You like that?"

"Yeah."

Fingertips glide up my thighs and under my dress. He palms my ass, grinding me against him. This was a brilliant wardrobe choice. The steel outline of his dick teases my clit through the thin fabric of panties. I press down and circle my hips. Finn moans, easing me back and forth. If he keeps this up, I'm going to come. It's been so long. *He's* so long.

He nips and bites his way down my neck, and as much as I don't want to, I somehow find the strength to say the words recommended by the dating gurus of the interweb: "We should stop."

He halts immediately, but his chest rises and falls in ragged movements. "Sorry. I couldn't control myself."

"No, it's okay." I untangle myself and return to the passenger side.

He rakes a hand through his hair, adjusts himself, and walks me to the door. We kiss again, long and slow, but I don't invite him in.

When I climb into bed, I can't help but think, maybe Charlotte was right about the opposite theory after all. Only for a millisecond did I imagine he was Austin.

FIVE

STUDIES SHOW that couples who sweat together, stay together. I should be searching for a new place right now. Instead, I'm standing in the SuperFit gym, in my super uncomfortable Spanx-style leggings, staring at a list of exercises scrawled on a chalkboard, wondering if it's too late to fake sick.

You can't tell me a man didn't come up with these names—burpees, snatch, wall balls, clean jerks? None of which I'm certain I can complete, much less the required number.

When Finn invited me here, I was still riding the high of our make-out session. Of course, *anyone* making out with Finn's abs would have made this mistake. Surely I can do something on this list. I'm in reasonable shape. There's a decent amount of lifting and whatnot I do at my job. The clay slabs are five pounds apiece, so I can't possibly embarrass myself *too* much.

"Chloe?" a feminine voice says from behind me.

I turn to see Austin's girlfriend.

"Lucy, hi." She's not dressed for a workout, unless she does so in trousers and heels. "What are you doing here?"

"I had a meeting with the owner to discuss PR for the gym. He'd like to franchise it."

Lucy is only five years older than me, yet I feel she's ten years ahead as far as accomplishing life goals. No wonder Austin is with her. She's already a vice president. I just have vices.

"I didn't know you work out at SuperFit," she adds.

"Well, I don't. My guy friend works here and is giving me a training session today."

Her blue eyes widen. "Your guy friend? Guy friend as in boyfriend?"

"No, he's not my boyfriend. Just kind of dating. It's still really new."

"Are you exclusive?"

Well, hm. That's a great question. It hadn't crossed my mind whether Finn is handing out rocks to other women. Are people on dating apps monogamous once you go on more than one date? The pro-tip article said couples take up to eight dates to declare themselves exclusive. I kind of figured there was an honor system here, but now I don't know.

"It's still really new," I repeat.

This is all so strange to discuss with Lucy. We barely know each other. Finn and I barely know each other.

Think of the devil and he'll arrive. Finn saves me from further inquisition. "Hey, you."

He snakes an arm around my waist and pulls me flush for a peck on the lips. Lucy handles his lack of PDA restraint as if he just shook my hand. Of course, Austin does use handcuffs, so this is probably quite tame on her dominatrix scale.

I introduce Lucy and then the worst thing happens.

"I have a wild question," she says. "Can I join your session? It'll give me creativity for the marketing campaign."

"Sure," Finn says. "You can change in the locker room."

"I have clothes in my car. Give me ten minutes and I'll be back."

Her heels tap-tap away and I give Finn my best faux smile. I'm not keen on Lucy joining us. Mostly for selfish reasons. This was more so an opportunity to see Finn in his habitat, with flirty touches, but now, with Lucy in the mix, I'll have to put in real effort. Well, there's nothing to do here, except go with it. And that's what I do when Lucy and her toned body returns. Somehow, in blue yoga pants that stop at her knees and a matching sports bra, she manages to look glamorous.

"Let's do this," she says.

We follow Finn through the rows of treadmills and stationary bikes to a semi-secluded area in the back of the gym.

"Okay, ladies. This workout will be intense." He rolls out two blue yoga mats. "It'll test your endurance and strength, so it's important to stretch properly."

"Sounds ominous," I joke. Sort of.

We sit, legs splayed, and follow Finn's guidance. I'm not going to lie, stretching *is* a mini-workout for me. A mirrored wall behind Finn refuses to let me stop comparing myself to Lucy. She's graceful as a swan as she rests her head on her knee and touches the tips of her toes. I'm a duckling who rests my head on my chest and touches my knees.

After five minutes of loosening our limbs, Finn declares it "go time."

He pops up and drags a box to the middle of our space.

"Watch me," he says. His muscles ripple as he

demonstrates how to do a two-footed jump onto it and then off, five times.

This move is easy—for Lucy. I've become a faulty kangaroo. The box is just high enough to make it difficult to catch my balance.

"Good job, babe," Finn says, when I land the last one with a grunt. "Balls to the wall."

He tosses us each a red ball. Guess who doesn't catch theirs? After I've retrieved mine, he shows us what this exercise involves. Like a trained athlete, he rises from a deep squat position, before racing to a line taped on the wall, soaring into the air, and slapping his ball at least a foot above it. Any other time, I'd marvel at the glimpses of skin, the impressive calf muscles, the way his gym shorts hang on his hips...that time is not now.

I've been designated to go first. Even though they've been stretched, my legs aren't prepared to spring out of a squat and run. In an awkward lunge, I stumble a bit and drop my ball.

"You got this, Chloe," Lucy says.

Although her sportsmanship is kind, no, I really don't. The second, third, and fourth try isn't easier. The fifth time, I throw my ball at the wall.

"Woo-hoo," I say. "Hit the target."

Finn laughs. "Let's go, Lucy."

While she slams her ball against the wall with

ease, I grab a towel to mop the tsunami from my forehead while Finn's distracted.

"Is the air even on in here?" I mutter to myself. Exercising is making me grumpy. I'm more of a walk outdoors and enjoy the scenery kind of girl. You know, the kind of exercise I look cute doing.

"Dumbbell snatches are next," Finn says.

I'm hoping that wasn't an insult.

Once again, we're squatting. For masochism, ten pound weights in each hand have been added to the mix. Sweat runs in rivers down my face as I do my best to keep up. For real, where's the air conditioning? An article I read this morning said this is a great way to be in tune with your partner. Said it promotes bonding. Mm-hmm. Sure. Grown-ups *are* liars. Lucy and Finn are in sync, touching their dumbbells to the floor and rising, while I'm the stray whack-a-mole popping up a few seconds too late.

When Finn finally calls it complete, Lucy says, "I'm loving this."

I'm too busy catching my breath to commit murder.

Weirdly, Finn just smiles before re-focusing on me. It's a little surprising that he isn't at all put off by my performance. In fact, he's kind of like a small child wanting to show off his prowess.

Speaking of small children, it turns out that a

burpee is *not* me sitting on Finn's lap while he gently caresses my back.

"You're kidding, right?" I ask when he completes a four part push-up move.

Narrator: *he was not kidding.*

"Show me what you're made of, Chloe," he responds.

Well, it's not sugar and spice and everything nice. More like Jell-O and spite. Lucy and I are to do these ridiculous burpees at the same time, and I'm cursing up a storm in my head when he starts chanting, "Squat. Pop. Stand. Reach."

Lucy's ponytail circles like a lasso as she does the quick succession of movements. Around the halfway mark, I skip the push-up and invent a new move—the Chloe-e. I squat, clap, and then complete the rest.

"You're doing awesome," Finn lies. Badly. "One more exercise and you're done."

Hallelujah. As we move to the weight benches in the corner, he makes sure to show how heavy his weights are, and tells us he's just set a new personal record for deadlifts.

"That's impressive," I tell him. I mean it, too. This is hard as shit and he makes it look easy.

When he's occupied with spotting Lucy, I try to get my panting under control. Like my life, I have mixed success. Hands on hips, I watch as Lucy breathes through several reps, barely straining her biceps. She's good at everything. Much too soon, she lowers the bar to its resting position with a jarring clank, and now it's my turn. I straddle the bench parallel to the one Lucy used and lean back onto the stiff leather padding. I'm ecstatic for the chance to lie down for a few minutes.

Finn makes adjustments to the weights, and I grip the cool metal bar.

"On the count of three," he says. "Lift it over your head and remember to keep your arms straight."

"I'm *so* tired."

"Don't give up, Chloe. You're so close," Lucy says. "How badly do you want it?"

Not much. I'm on the fence about which is worse, this workout or having the girlfriend of the guy I thought was my twin flame encouraging me. Why must she be so nice?

"You got this. You're stronger than you think," Finn says, looking down on me.

I'm sure this fiasco is the end of our journey. That article said happiness is contagious and it's hard to walk away from happy people. Negativity is one of the biggest turn-offs. Well, the only thing I'm positive about right now—I am not happy. A man who does this *every day* must want someone like Lucy. She's happy. She's smiling right now.

Regardless, I'm not one to give up. I flex and lift the bar and by the grace of God it doesn't fall back down on me. It's not so bad after all. Huh. I really am stronger than I think. This may be my favorite. Perhaps I was a weight lifter in another life. Perhaps we don't end here after all. Perhaps I finally impressed Mr. Personal Record.

When I finish the last rep, Finn winks at me. "Do you feel SuperFit?"

"Sure." I swing my legs off the bench.

"This was amazing," Lucy says, dabbing her face with a towel. "You're a phenomenal instructor. Thanks for letting me join."

"Any time," Finn says. "You did awesome."

She gives me a hug which only demonstrates again that I sweat and she glows, whispering, "He's a keeper."

"Is he?" I've spent so much time trying to do everything right, that I've had no time to focus on whether he's wrong for me.

She pulls me off to the side, while Finn tidies up the space. "He put dummy weights on your bar."

"Dummy weights?"

"Yeah, zero weights." She tosses her towel over a shoulder. "I better get going and back to the office. Let's do this again. Austin isn't a gym person."

She flounces away and Finn moves in front of me.

He holds out a bottled water. "That was a great workout."

"For you," I say, with only the mildest amount of sarcasm. The very mildest. I chug the ice-cold drink and bid a fond farewell to my weightlifting dreams.

"I can't believe I got anything done while you were there, looking so hot. When you squatted...damn, Chloe. It was torture."

The fiery look in his eyes tells me he's serious. I'm sweaty. Disheveled. Still haven't caught my breath. And I'm walking sort of strange due to the fact that my legs aren't exactly holding me up the way they once did, six years ago, before this workout started. I don't even want to think about what I smell like. *This* is hot to him?

"What are you doing at three o'clock?" he asks.

"Resting?"

"I need you at three o'clock."

I drain the rest of my water to stall. I like him. I do. But I have nothing left to give after this workout. It's possible I can muster something up from within my exhausted body. He did take pity on me and switch out my weights. "What do you need me for?"

Once again, he doesn't tell me, he shows me by

gripping my hips and snapping me against his groin. He's hard.

Welp. Okay. Just to make sure we're on the same page, I whisper, "Sexy times?"

He nods. Ah, three o'clock is the dicking hour. This is technically date three, so sex is okay, but now I have doubts. Lucy's exclusivity question, for one. But you know, I'm not going to fixate on that. I'm an adult, so I'm going to enjoy a hot shower and let him ravage me.

After all those burpees, I *deserve* this.

SIX

EVEN THOUGH SUPERFIT WAS A SUPERSHITSHOW, I'm stoked for SuperSex. I've spent the last hour mentally preparing. Opening myself up—literally—is a tremendous step. I've picked apart all the possible outcomes. Nothing seems horrendous enough to prevent going through with the sexy times.

Sure, I'd like to know Finn better on an intellectual and emotional level. But sexual compatibility is also important in a relationship. If you think about it, there must be hordes of dissatisfied women out there, faking orgasms, who wish they'd taken a test drive. So I'm willing to sacrifice my current nun-like state of grace to avoid that particular hell later. If the whole world will stop texting, that is.

Hey, Gran! Can I call you later? I text back to my grandmother's third message.

IT'S IMPORTANT, CHLOE, she replies in all caps. No matter how many times I've tried to explain why people consider this yelling, she's too stubborn to care.

Is it about Ruth?

It's always about Ruth and their endless neighborly feud.

YES. SHE BROUGHT LEMON PIE TO THE POTLUCK. SHE KNOWS THAT'S MY THING.

I pinch the bridge of my nose and remind myself this woman raised me, and no dick will ever trump that. Even if the dick will be here soon.

No way! I'm sure it wasn't as good as yours.

IT WAS TOO TART. AND THE MERINGUE WAS FLAT. I'VE PUT THE TEN COMMANDMENTS ON OUR PROPERTY LINE TO REMIND THAT TART NOT TO COVET WHAT OTHERS HAVE. LEMON PIE IS MINE.

You're a badass, Gran.

I'VE GOT TO GO. CALL ME LATER. LOVE YOU.

Love you, too.

Charlotte receives the next reply. From the assortment of flowers she's sent for my opinion, I prefer the lily for her bridal bouquet. The Friends-OfFriends notifications get ignored. Since meeting Finn, I haven't even glanced at any of the new requests. I'm a singular focused gal. Rather, I'm trying to be. The next message gives me a lurch in my belly, like I just took a plunge down a steep incline on a roller coaster.

Austin.

"You haven't been around. I need my history. What do you have for me today?"

My thumbs ache to fly across the keyboard and give him a tidbit. I fear that would be counterproductive in moving on from my unrequited crush. Right? To play devil's advocate, we are friends. He's unaware of the pedestal I have him on, so it's not fair to shun him because of my issues.

The text stares at me, waiting for my decision. I sigh. Why do the right people come along at the wrong time? So many times I've wondered what it would be like to be loved by Austin, but I don't even know what real love feels like. Books and movies show what it's supposed to be, and so far, I haven't experienced the mythical phenomenon. It's not his fault I have these thoughts. It's a messy situation.

And on that note, I reply, "Originally, tablecloths were designed as a communal napkin."

There. With every ounce of willpower I possess, Austin is pushed into the far recesses of my mind and barricaded, so he can't escape to wreak havoc on my time with Finn. Lucy said Finn was a keeper, and she has Austin, so she must know something I don't.

The doorbell rings as I place my phone on the kitchen counter. My feet float across the hardwoods on my way to the door. When I open it, Finn reaches for me, hoisting me up as if I'm weightless.

"Hi," I say, wrapping my legs around his waist.

With his warm hands supporting my ass, he walks me inside and kicks the door closed.

"I want you so bad," he says.

Nose to nose, I ask, "How bad?"

Again, he's excellent at showing and not telling. There's no time to give him a tour of anything, except my mouth. On a growl, he captures my bottom lip with his teeth, then slides his tongue inside. It's all so hot. So new.

No man has ever carried me before. I'm not even concerned whether I'm heavy. Much.

My back thumps against the wall.

Yesss.

All my experiences have been in the prone position, and I exhale a breathy moan at the mere thought of wall sex. Goosebumps fan across my shoulder when he tears his lips from mine and sucks his way down my neck. With a wriggle of my knees, I inch his shorts down.

"You ready for me, babe?"

"Mm-hmm. Right here. Against the wall."

Through the thin cotton of my tank, he bites a nipple. "You're a dirty girl, huh?"

Maybe I am. This is uncharted territory. Finn doesn't know me well enough to know I'm figuring myself out, so I throw caution to the wind and embellish my inner slut. "I'm filthy."

The low rumble in his throat voices his approval. "I knew you were going to be a wildcat when I met you."

Well, that's interesting. I'm curious what vibe I exuded that made him think that about me, but his hips bump and grind all the wayward thoughts out of my head.

"I'm going to make you purr like a kitten."

Not to seem picky, but I'd have preferred something more powerful. I want to roar like a lioness. But again, he does this magic trick with his tongue and that errant thought too vanishes into the ether. In the middle of another searing kiss, he spins from my happy place against the wall and deposits me on the couch. Bummer. My disappointment at the new location morphs to wide-eyed wonder as he whisks his T-shirt off…and carefully folds it.

It's odd he took time to do that, but a neat man is good. At least I know he isn't likely to leave a trail of dirty laundry in every room.

"I can't wait to taste you." In a flash, his greedy hands remove my shorts and panties. Precisely folded, they join his T-shirt on the end table. "Open up for me."

"Here?" The urge to cross my legs is stronger than Finn and his dead lifts. Even with the blinds closed, the room is too bright.

"Yeah, babe." His impressive cock tents the front of his shorts, and you know, who cares? Vitamin D is good for the immune system, they say. Eager to see what oral skills he possesses, I settle back in the cushions and spread.

"Mm, fuck." He drops between my thighs, and trails a finger along my seam. "Ah, so wet."

With a slow drag of his tongue, any lingering insecurities dissolve. The only thing that matters are the erotic sounds he makes as he feasts on me. There is no inch of my pussy he doesn't explore. I brace my feet on his shoulders and ride the wave of sensations cascading throughout my body.

As he nips and sucks, my fingers delve into his thick hair, holding him captive. At the perfect pace and pressure, he circles my clit until I'm bucking off the couch.

"Yes, just like that." I've never been with such a voracious man. Even his nose is in on the action. "Oh my God, don't stop."

A sublime tingle starts in my toes and works its way up my legs, spreading all the way to the top of my head. When he slips a finger inside, the tight wire coiled in my belly unfurls until my whole body buzzes with electric currents.

My back arches and I come all over his face.

When the shudders subside, I'm definitely purring.

My not-yet-recovered body is pulled to standing. From his lips come the most decadent sentence, "Taste how sweet you are."

Our kiss is hungry and leaves me starving for more. I may need him to satisfy me again. Just to be double sure we're compatible. He has other plans.

From his pocket, he produces the mysterious brush he purchased at my work. "I want you to paint me."

I tilt my head. "Like a portrait?"

"No. My body."

A little unexpected foreplay. None of the articles expanded on third date sex and where the boundaries lie. There must not be any.

"Okay," I say. "Be right back."

Bare-assed, I tug my tank down and hustle to the laundry room. Tubes of paint littering the shelves fly as I scramble through them to find blue and red. I snatch a mini palette, a towel too, and dash back to Finn.

A now-nude Finn.

My pace slows as I take in the lean muscles and surreal etches before me. The v accentuating his hips is phenomenal, as if someone hand-carved his beautiful body.

"Wow," I murmur. He's like a Rodin sculpture come-to-life, full of ferocious emotion, in need of no decoration. An x-rated work of art, of course. There's a monumental difference in genitalia.

"Where do you want me?" he says, in a throaty voice.

Inside me, but patience is a virtue. "Um..." I glance around the room and this is bad, but I can't ruin the furniture with stray paint splatters. I need my deposit back to use toward the next place. "Standing is good."

I spread the towel out and drop down, one knee and then the other, before him.

He fists his cock, stroking. "This is so fucking sexy."

God, it is. But he's a wild card who might choose

to have sex on top of the chair. With moving out looming over my head, I need to carefully consider which parts to paint. Most of the furnishings belong to June, and I'm not sure she'd appreciate heathen body smears all over it.

While I ponder where to start my masterpiece, it's hard to look away from the sensual movement of his hand and the way he's enjoying it. My heart bangs against my chest as I squeeze paint onto the palette and dip my brush in blue. Where to start? I study him and decide to paint his manscaped balls. Not only do they seem least problematic, they're an erogenous zone.

"Oh, yeah," he says, when the brush touches him. It's hard to concentrate on what I'm doing as he tugs at his dick. The way he grips the thickness, stroking from root to tip, is the most erotic thing I've ever seen. His well-defined thighs clench as he pleasures himself to my artistry.

When I swirl a red *s* onto the blue base, he hisses and jerks off at a rapid pace.

"Fuck, I need inside you."

The brush falls from my hand as he raises me from my kneeling position. In a blur of Superman balls, he flies to the shorts folded on the table and removes a condom. It's rolled on faster than I can blink. He stalks back, and again lifts me.

I cling to his broad shoulders. "Against the wall," I plead, equals parts aroused and afraid he'll go for the couch.

My request is granted. The head of his cock eases in, and ah, God. We groan together as I acclimate to his size. His forehead drops to mine.

With a hand braced on the wall, he pumps into me.

"You're so tight," he says.

Over and over.

And over.

In varying forms as he takes me to the clouds—

"You're so tight, Chloe."

"Damn, you're tight."

"Tight as fuck."

"So. Tight."

To make it stop, I kiss him. I'm soaring to my destination, faster than the speed of light. I'm on cruise control.

"Feel good, babe?"

"Yes," I whimper. He's bendy and has stamina, ramming in and out, until I'm a quivering mass of limbs.

"Come on me," he demands when my orgasm can no longer be contained.

It's glorious, and breathtaking, and my first from

penetration. Finn's release quickly follows mine with an exquisite jerk of his body.

He doesn't stay over afterward, but he leaves me with a kiss and a promise to call. I'm not necessarily smitten, but I'm damn sure satisfied, and isn't that a good place to start?

SEVEN

"IS FINN LOST?" Charlotte asks.

"Just running late. Busy Saturday at the gym," I say, dropping my phone into my handbag. "He's in the parking lot."

While we wait for him to join us, people move around us in droves at the Spring Thing Bazaar. It's *the* craft fair of the season, and I should know—I'm a craft fair whore.

Charlotte's brown eyes hold a hint of laughter. "I still can't believe you painted his balls. They're the least sexy part. Like, what guy wants his balls painted?"

As all best friends do, I filled Charlotte in on the pertinent details of my afternoon tryst with Finn. To respect his privacy, I should have left out that minor detail, but it turned into a major thing. In my haste to pleasure him, I didn't really take into consideration the paint removal process. When Finn called later that night to ask how to remove it without also removing his delicate skin, panic ensued. To his credit, he was a good sport and said blue balls were accurate until the next time he was with me.

"In his defense, he just said paint him. I picked his balls."

Smiling, she moves to a steel column and studies the location directory of the one hundred-plus vendors. "Think Finn has the stamina for the craft fair?"

The better question is, do I? The bazaar is an open style warehouse, covering an acre of land. Under normal circumstances, you pretty much have to haul me out of here. Today, they may have to do it on a stretcher.

"Honestly, I can barely walk." It's been three days since our sexcapades, and I'm still not recovered.

"I'm going to tell my fiancé we need to christen every wall in our new house."

"Do it at your own risk. I think wall sex broke me."

A cough interrupts our discussion. "I uh...got kettle corn," Austin says.

The sudden whoosh of blood pounding in my

ears silences the chatter of the crowd around us. How much of our conversation did he hear? I'd like to crawl under the display table of colorful gnomes, but I force my lips upward and pretend nothing is amiss.

"Oh, yum." I take a piece and pop it in my mouth. It's no big deal he overheard us talking about sex. First of all, I wasn't bragging. Or exaggerating. My legs are so sore, it was excruciating slipping on my jeans and boots today. Second of all, I'm over him —or working towards it. But it's always good to distract...

"Did you know, at one time, the wealthy would hire people to be ornamental hermits that lived in their gardens?"

He glances at the garden gnomes watching us and rewards me with a half-grin. "That may be the most disturbing fact you've ever given me."

"You're welcome." I take another piece of warm popcorn and smile. "Isn't it nice to know there's always a backup plan if life doesn't really work out?"

"So where is this Fitbit guy?" he says, choosing to ignore any possibility of garden life.

As I chew, I focus on the indent between his dark brows.

"Finn," I correct. "He'll be here any minute."

"Hide your kryptonite, people," Charlotte says. "I think SuperFinn has arrived."

It's a nickname I know he'll never shed when I turn to see Finn striding toward us, wearing jeans and an actual Superman T-shirt. I give a wave, while warring butterflies battle it out in my stomach. He's so handsome, but will my friends like him? It's important to me they do, because after the sex, I sort of want this to work with Finn. I'm invested. The swoony butterflies win when he reaches us and handles the introductions with dazzling charm. All that's missing is a Mr. Clean-style sparkling tooth when he shakes their hands.

"So you're a Superman fan?" Charlotte asks.

"Well, he is the Man of Steel," Finn says, with a wink. For a moment, I'm fearful he'll flex.

"I just wrote a piece on personality types and your favorite superheroes for the psychology magazine I work for," she tells him.

"Ah. What does mine say about me?"

Charlotte launches into an in-depth analysis, and I latch onto the last part of what she says, "You're loyal and ready to save the day." Oh, interesting. Loyal is good. "You don't like to lose." Yep, I could see this after the nine-plate buffet.

"I'll take it," he says.

"My fiancé is a Spiderman guy," Charlotte tells him. "It fits him. Completely responsible with a dash of nerdy."

"Everyone knows Batman is the best," Austin adds.

Finn chuckles. "We'll have to agree to disagree on that one, man."

Austin arches a brow, and tosses a handful of kettle corn in his mouth. This superhero thing might become volatile, so I defuse the situation. "Ready to look around and have some judgy fun?"

Finn drapes an arm over my shoulders. "Lead the way, babe."

Our quartet ambles into the flow of people and a few feet down, Charlotte stops at an enormous patch of ceramic bunnies in an array of sizes.

"Ah, the season's hottest trend," I say, moving from under Finn's shoulder to gawk at the variety of pudgy rabbits.

Austin picks up a tan bunny with long ears and jumbo feet. "Uh-oh. This one appears to have a hare-line fracture."

I laugh and wish I didn't enjoy his corny jokes so much.

Finn moves beside me. "What kind of person makes only bunnies?" He glances at the silver-haired woman ringing up a sale.

"Lots of people stick to a particular item," I tell him. "But this craft fair is seasonal, so a lot of vendors will focus on whatever holiday is upcoming."

"Plus, she might be onto something," Charlotte says. "Look at her line. It's hopping."

Finn smiles at her pun and so far, it's going well. I'm noticing I never say *great*. Except for the sex. Minus the tight thing, sex was great, so we're definitely compatible in that area. Hopefully, we are in others. Like friends.

This morning, I read introducing your inner circle is a serious step in a relationship. This is a casual relaxed atmosphere like they recommended, so why am I so on edge? Maybe it's the clowns Finn is now entranced with across the aisle. It's a horrid display of white-painted faces with cherry noses and creepy smiles. Their creator, a bald man with a bushy mustache, engages Finn in conversation. The surrounding cacophony prevents me from hearing what they're discussing and why Finn is so enthralled. My phone buzzes.

Dude, if he buys a fucking clown, I'm not okay, a message from Charlotte reads.

I quickly reply, ***Not everyone hates clowns.***

You do! I do! All the people murdered by them do!

I can't believe I'm about to say this, but... ***#Notallclowns***

Name one.

Ronald McDonald.

She doesn't look convinced.

Another message arrives from Austin. It's two emojis—a clown and a knife.

"Stop. They can't all be bad. Did you know there are clown commandments?"

"I did not know this," he replies. "Is *thou shalt not kill* not one of them?"

"Babe," Finn calls, "come here a minute."

Somehow, I force my feet over to him. "What's up?"

"Carl here says there's a clown motel in Nevada. Next to a graveyard. How cool would that be for Halloween?"

My phone nearly rockets out of my pocket from the vibrations. But more important, he's making future plans. "Oh, hm. That might be a little too spooky for me."

"I'll protect you," he says, grinning.

"Yeah, no."

"Thanks for helping with the box," Carl says to Finn. "Would've dropped it, if you hadn't swooped in."

Aw. Carl leaves to assist another customer, and the breath stuck in my lungs leaves in a rush when Finn turns away, empty-handed. We rejoin Austin and Charlotte, and the clown crisis is averted when I send them both a text letting them know Finn was only saving the day for Carl.

We mosey further through the fair, and around the midway mark, near the crocheted rabbits, I sense Finn's interest waning. He stands with his shoulder propped against a life-size Easter Bunny, checking his phone, while we study the intricate tapestries hanging from hooks.

"I think Finn is bored," Charlotte whispers to me.

Discreetly, I tug her far enough away for Austin not to hear. "Do you think he fits?"

"It only matters if you think he does. Now that I know he's not a clown killer, I can see the appeal."

That's not a winning endorsement, but I'll take it.

We continue on to the next section, and Finn engages with my friends in lighthearted conversation as we weave in and out of a plethora of kitchen products.

"When are you going to put up a table, Chloe?" Charlotte asks.

"Yeah. You should do it for the summer fair," Austin says.

They're always supportive of my art, encouraging me to put up a table of my own, instead of just critiquing all the shabby pottery from other artists. But hey, judging is half the fun.

I shrug. "I don't know. I don't know if it would sell."

"What do you want to sell?" Finn asks.

"Well, I have a whole vision of my products." I tell him all about my plans for Mae'd With Love. My wares will consist of a variety of handmade and hand-painted kitchen items. Each will include a recipe, printed on a keepsake recipe card, from Granny Mae's delicious and extensive repertoire.

Pie plates for her heavenly lemon pie.

Serving bowls for her creamy mashed potatoes.

I'll start small and then expand into dishes, mugs, platters. She has a million recipes, and I have a million ideas.

"I like it, babe." He kisses my forehead. "You're cute. All that talk of food made me hungry." He looks over at the nearby dining area. "Want to grab something to eat?"

I'm not sure what I was expecting or if I'm expecting too much, but I'm cute? Austin said my plan was brilliant, not that I'm comparing. I'm totally comparing, and need to stop. I shrug off his lackluster reply and agree.

Our group crosses to the concession window

where a smiling brunette takes our order. When she hands Finn a number, he says, "Thanks, babe."

My gaze shoots to him. Hm. Okay. It never crossed my mind that babe could be a general term he used. It's like my grandmother calling everyone "hun." I'm not sure how I feel about this discovery. Well, I am. I just don't want to admit my disappointment that I'm not special.

When we have our food, we join Austin and Charlotte at a picnic table. While I stew on the fact my endearment was not in fact an endearment, Finn pulls something from his pocket. I'm praying it's not another paintbrush.

"While you were looking at the garden stuff, I got this for you." He hands me a palm-sized stone, painted with a dandelion and the word *wish*. "I thought with the whole rock thing, you'd like it."

My chest clenches, and the babe thing is no longer important. Just look at this. "It's so perfect. Thank you."

"That's pretty sweet, Finn," Charlotte says. "Mine needs to up his game before the wedding."

Finn asks when the big day is and as Charlotte gives him the details, my phone vibrates.

That's cute and all, but your boyfriend should only be calling you babe. I look up and meet Austin's dark stare before he's drawn into their conversation.

When Charlotte brings up moving out, Austin mentions he still needs a new roommate. And then, like a clown rolling up to a party, the worst thing happens.

"Oh, yeah? I'm in the market," Finn says. "Ideally, I'd like to buy a place, but I might be interested."

I almost choke on my fry. I make a mental note, in bold letters, to talk him out of that idea. There definitely won't be any getting over Austin if my boyfriend is sleeping in his house.

Not that Finn is my boyfriend. Not that I want him to be my boyfriend. Not that I know what I want at all.

But, really, does anybunny?

EIGHT

"Dating is about finding out who you are and who others are. If you show up in a masquerade outfit, neither is going to happen."— Henry Cloud, *How to Get a Date Worth Keeping*

YOU'RE A WISE ONE, Henry. I bookmark the site, so I can come back later. My boyfriend is here. A few days ago, at a celebration after his SuperFit competition, Finn introduced me as his girlfriend to a competitor. So it's official; we're a couple. Dating advice is now a thing of the past. I've graduated to relationship articles, and the site I'm on says couples who cuddle together, stay together. Tonight we're going to watch a show, because I can't even imagine going out with my quads like this.

When I open the door, Finn, glorious against the backdrop of a tangerine and violet sky, frowns. "You aren't dressed."

I glance down at my joggers and T-shirt. I did indeed remember pants. So... "I'm dressed."

He steps inside. "You're wearing pajamas?"

"Lounge wear."

"How fast can you get ready?"

"Like...making popcorn ready? I didn't think you'd want any."

He chuckles. "Like *clothes*. For the show we're going to?"

Ah, it appears there's been a misunderstanding about the type of show. "It's um"—I wink—"like Netflix-and-chill kind of show."

Emphasis on the "chill" part. Finn and I haven't had sex since the blue balls. The taxing mental preparation for the SuperFit competition apparently required no surplus energy be expelled in bedroom activities. After he won, I thought he'd throw me over his shoulder caveman style. I was wrong. Once the celebration ended, he needed to rest his muscles.

"Sitting around all night?" he asks. "That's not really my vibe."

It's my *whole* vibe, so that's concerning.

I follow him into the living room. "It'll be romantic."

"Babydoll."

Since we're now a couple, I'm babydoll. So there was no misunderstanding, I clarified this is a true pet name.

"You've been home all day," he says. "Let's go out. It's good to be flexible."

His boyish grin doesn't make a dent in my staying-in-tonight armor. I've gone with him to work out three times a week. That's six times in two weeks. That's more than I've done in my entire life. Plus, I've given up pasta. We never have dinner dates at Italian places, because his macro count rules his meal choices.

I'm definitely flexible.

I even look the other way when he gets more waxes than I do, so no hair will distract from the clean lines of his muscles. And let's not forget the couple's tanning date last week. The least romantic thing ever. I have zero desire for couple's melanoma later on. I tipped my girl twenty dollars I couldn't afford to *not* turn my bed on.

I even decided to queue up *Jack Ryan* for tonight so that Finn won't have to suffer through deciphering the *Letterkenny* jokes my friends and I favor. So really, I've made an awful lot of concessions to *his vibe.* He can give me this. The whole reason I wanted to stay in was because his gym overworked my body.

"Well, I haven't been home all day. I had tea with June."

To remind myself of the chemistry between us, I step between his legs and press my lips to his. The spark flares immediately. Maybe I shouldn't complain about his regimen. At the competition, I discovered he wasn't even close to being the craziest SuperFit guy. Shocking as it is to consider, some people are much weirder, obsessive, and bizarrely even more muscular.

He squeezes my ass. "Okay, we'll stay in," he says.

"I'm going to open new worlds for you tonight," I promise.

After all, he really has shown me things too—working out is horrendous, but all my lower back pain from hunching over the potter's wheel is gone. I might not eat pasta with him, but who knew Japanese food was so good?

Streaming shows are universal. We can enjoy

this. It's all about compromise, according to the relationship experts.

"Get comfy," I tell him. "It's good to relax."

He picks my favorite spot on the right end of the sofa, but that's okay. I'm flexible. I dim the lights and settle beside him with my legs stretched, feet propped on the coffee table. It's cozy with his arm draped along the back of the couch. If I laser focus on the television, his hand tapping the cushion doesn't bother me at all.

Ten minutes in, when Jack is taking a row on the Potomac, Finn rises from the couch. "All that water is making me thirsty. Mind if I get something to drink?"

I hit pause. "I'll grab you one. There's Vitamin Water in the fridge." That's another thing. My refrigerator is now stocked with healthy items. So again, he can give me this.

"No, you stay there." He beelines into the kitchen.

When he returns, I press play, and he remains standing, guzzling water, pacing like a lion trapped in a cage.

"You all right?"

"Yeah." Finally, he resumes his seat, and Jack, the stoic hero, is back in suspenseful action.

"Come on, man," he says to the TV. "You know he's the bad guy."

This type of commentary continues through the first half. Finn's not only a talker during TV-watching, he's a doer. He heads back to the kitchen. I pause again.

"Just grabbing more water," he calls out. "You could have let it play."

"You would have missed the clue." As have I. I'm sure if I could hear what they were saying, I'd know what was going on.

"I'm not a spy-thriller guy," he says. "But if you like it, we can watch it."

"I'm not into it either." The whole point is to find something we both enjoy doing. "What do you like to watch?"

"I don't watch a lot of TV." He sits. "When I do, it's more real-life action stuff that doesn't follow a script. *Bear Grylls. American Ninja Warrior.* Ever seen *Floor Is Lava?*"

"Nope."

I offer him the remote and Jack disappears from the screen. He's replaced by a game show that involves teams of three making it through a wonky house to challenge their strength and endurance.

"The floor isn't actually lava," he says.

"Don't spoil it," I joke, but then immediately regret. He might actually think I believe the producers could somehow transport molten lava into the studio.

He kisses the tip of my nose. "Sorry."

As the contestants leap and travel across the basement, Finn shouts animated play-by-play like an announcer. It's giving me flashbacks to the gym. In episode four, they attempt to swing through a booby-trapped kitchen on steroids.

"Think you could make it through that?" Finn asks. "We could try out for it."

My eye twitches. "Well, we'd need a third person."

"Maybe Austin. He seems like he'd be a good competitor," Finn says.

His phone chimes, saving me from responding. And really, I don't have one.

He types away for a few minutes and then says, "My buddy knows a guy who has a place available, if I want to take a look at it. Says it's a hot property that'll go fast."

"Oh, that's great."

"Want to come with me? Give the feminine perspective."

"Now?"

"Yeah."

"Sure."

This is technically not going out. It's a spontaneous house hunt, so he doesn't end up with Austin. And there's always the chance it will give me some ideas on areas for my own move. So far, repeated searches have returned nothing within my meager price range. Lucky for me, June hasn't had any interested buyers yet, but that could change at any moment.

We drive east, about fifteen minutes outside of Boulder, to a secluded community with a perfect view of the Flatirons. The GPS leads us down a tree-lined road to an expanse of land surrounding a miniature wood house with a tall glass front.

I lean toward the windshield and gawk at the structure illuminated by the truck's headlights. "It's a tiny house."

"No way," he says. "I'm not paying three thousand a month for a dollhouse."

"Three thousand?" I shriek.

"Yeah. Mike said it's an engineer who owns it. It's actually a vacation rental, but they'll do a long-term lease."

"Well, we should at least check it out? They can be spacious inside."

"Okay, let's do it."

We exit and follow the lighted pathway to a cozy covered porch. Finn stoops and retrieves a key concealed beneath a planter beside the front door.

Inside, he flips on the lights and I'm in awe. It's beautiful. But incredibly small. The camera angles must make them appear larger. Even with the high ceilings and glass wall, Finn dwarfs the interior.

"Yeah, not happening," he says, scanning the probably seven hundred square feet.

I scoot around him to explore.

"It's so fascinating how they find hidden storage for all the things that you need." I turn a handle on the wall and a dining table comes down. "See. Isn't that amazing?"

"Babydoll, this *is* amazing. If you're a munchkin."

Ugh. There's no denying the lack of livable space, but he needs to be flexible enough to love this place. I mean, how fun would it be for *me* for my boyfriend to have a tiny house? Like a realtor, I point out all the positive aspects. Built-in bookshelf over the door. Storage beneath the couch cushions. No cords anywhere. They've made it luxurious and modern with dark hardwoods, and granite countertops in the minimalist kitchen.

"I'm not composting a toilet," he says, while I stand in the shower to show him a person can indeed fit. Sadly, there would never be shower sex, but sometimes you have to make sacrifices.

I step out, losing hope I'll change his mind. "I

think that's an incinerator toilet. It lights your...you know...on fire, in a totally safe way."

He gives me a flat look. "Light my shit on fire? Do I even need to say it?"

"No."

I'm still determined, when we leave the bathroom. In the loft area is the bedroom. I scramble up the narrow steps and duck my head to climb in the bed. "There's a skylight."

Finn peeks into the claustrophobic space. "Yeah, I'd have to stick my head out of it to fit in here."

This is true, but I'm not giving up. In a bit of a Houdini move, I roll off the bed and hunch my way out of the room. Downstairs, I brush past Finn and open a door that leads to an oversized concrete patio full of furniture. Bingo.

"Wow, this is huge." He follows me outside. "Your space is expanded outdoors." I spread my arms. "Endless entertaining back here under the stars."

He looks up at the night sky and doesn't seem dazzled by the multitude of twinkling dots.

Short chunks of wood lie stacked next to the house, so I try another tactic. "There's even a fire pit, for when it's chilly. Don't you want to live in harmony with nature?"

"Not really. Is Austin's place still available?"

This can't happen. Not to be negative, but what if there's a breakup? Who gets Austin? "I don't really think you want to room with Austin. He's a chef, so there's a constant temptation of delicious carbs."

"He seems laid-back, though. That's important."

"He is, but I don't think it's a good idea. Ya know?"

"Why not?" He moves closer and caresses my arms. "You thinking about maybe us living together?" he asks.

"Jesus, no." Oops. Too adamant. His question has me off-kilter. I wish I'd paid more attention to Jack Ryan tracking down clues. Is Finn leaving me a set as well? Is he more into this than I am? When I mentally advance to the future with Finn, it's blurry.

"I mean, just feels a little soon, right?" I say, softly. "It's only been a couple of weeks."

He nods. "So if I move in with him, you won't be hurt?"

I worry at the corner of my lip. How do I answer his question? I don't.

"Funny you should say hurt." Disregarding Henry's internet relationship advice, I slip on a mask. "I'm really sore from the workout yesterday. Maybe you could kiss it better?"

"YOU'RE MAKING ME HORNY," Finn says.

Success. My house of cards is still standing. Of course, guilt is now threatening to knock it down. But the primal way he's looking at me is now making me horny.

"Want to head back to my place?" I suggest.

"No. Here. Outside."

The staccato rhythm of his words is caveman-esque and sends an ache straight to my core. I've never had sex in the open, and the prospect excites me. There's a problem, though—this is someone else's property. It doesn't seem right to desecrate a stranger's patio.

Without uttering a word, Finn's tempting lips talk me into it. It's not like we're trespassing. He has a key, and we're not going to have sex in the tiny bed. We're outside.

"I'm in."

"Give me two minutes." In an impressive display that Bear Grylls would envy, he tosses logs into the basket-shaped fire pit and finds everything needed to bring it to life.

"See. You belong here."

He sits in an Adirondack chair, long legs spread. "Come here." I move in front of him. "Show me where it hurts."

I point to my bicep and he leans in, soothing the tender muscle with his lips. This turns into a sensual game where he nurtures every spot I direct him— inner thigh, hip, stomach, shoulder.

When I press a fingertip to my breast, he rubs the pad of his thumb against the stiff peak. "Are you going to be my dirty little slut tonight?"

Weirdly, I'm not offended by his words. Who am I? It's funny how you have no inkling what you like sexually until it's presented to you by a gorgeous man who follows it up with, "Only mine, though. No one else gets the dirty slut."

I nod, mesmerized by the shadow of flames dancing across his chiseled face. "I want you to do what I say, and then I'll make you come."

Oh, dear. What has been going on in the

bedrooms of America while I was making pottery? I feel so cheated by the beta males of my past.

"What do you want me to do?" Seems a fair question to ask. I'm learning to expect the unexpected with Finn.

"Take your clothes off," he says. "Let me see your body."

With lava—not real lava—coursing in my veins from his commanding tone, I tantalize him with an unhurried striptease. I've never stripped for a man before, but the roaring fire is making me hedonistic. Swaying to the imaginary music in my head, I inch my shirt up, exposing the skin beneath at a slow-moving pace. Once it's off, I let it flutter to the ground, and memorize every detail of Finn's reaction. The half grunt, the swipe of his tongue on his full lips, the rise of his chest.

My shoes are toed off, and I slip my fingertips in the waistband of my joggers and shimmy them off. Joggers aren't particularly sexy, but I feel sexy as I use them like a feather boa to finish my performance. When I'm done, I drop them with a wink.

His hooded gaze flickers to the pile by my feet, then burns a path over my white bra and panties. "You look like an angel."

Sparks fly from the crackle of fire, casting him in a devilish light. "You look very wicked."

"I'm going to spank you for not putting your clothes on the table. You like being spanked?"

It seems best to be truthful regarding something that involves pain. "I don't know. I've never been spanked, but I liked *Fifty Shades of Grey*." The, uh, movie. I didn't quite get around to the book.

"Turn around and bend over."

My pulse races. It's like all my constraints have disappeared without the confines of walls. Outdoors, I'm free as the rustle of wind in the trees. It's liberating.

With hands braced on my knees, I wiggle my bottom, eager to experience some light BDSM. For science.

I glance at him over my shoulder. "Ready when you are, Sir."

"Such a bad girl, showing off your thong." He smacks my ass. Not hard enough to hurt, but not a gentle tap either.

"Do you like that?" he asks, palming and massaging my cheek.

"I'll need another one to decide."

He gives me three more, each one stronger than the last. "You like it?"

The spanking itself isn't what's turning me on, it's the thrill of being naughty. "I like that you like it."

"You want to please me?"

"Yes." And I do. The unabashed desire he exudes for me is an aphrodisiac.

His finger slips inside my panties. "You're wet. Turn around."

My mouth waters as he lowers his zipper and eases his jeans and boxers past his hips. "Suck me, Chloe."

He wins bonus points for stealing the cushion from the chair next to him so I have a soft place to kneel. For the first time, I'm not intimidated about the prospect of giving a blowjob. I settle between his thighs ready to suck him like a porn star. He rubs the head of his cock against my lips, and I lick the tip, then swirl around the plump head. Once again, I focus on his balls, gently squeezing while I slide him into my mouth.

"Mmm." His fingers comb through my hair, until the loose strands are fisted in his hand. "I want to see you take all of me in your pretty mouth."

This is a daunting task, but a challenge I accept.

"Fuck, your mouth is so hot."

I'm enjoying his aural as much as he's enjoying my oral. I squeeze my thighs together and squirm from his raspy tone. There was a pro-tip I read in a magazine that said if you want to give an amazing blowjob he'll never forget, to suck and swirl. Emboldened by his responses, I test it out. It works. His guttural groan spurs me to take him deeper.

"Keep sucking," he says. "You're making me lose my mind."

His hips rock with urgency as my mouth and hand work in tandem, gliding up and down his velvet thickness. Even though I'm the one on my knees, I feel powerful. Like a goddess beneath the moonlight, worshipping Finn's dick.

"I'm going to come if you don't stop," he husks, leaving my mouth with a pop.

"Do it. Come in my mouth," I urge, because out here, under a blanket of dark, I'm a brave temptress.

"I want to come inside you."

Well, I can't deny him that. "I want that too."

He rises and sheds his clothes. My skills must've been phenomenal, because he doesn't bother to fold them before sheathing himself with a condom.

I'm scooped up and carried onto the cool lawn. It's prickly and hard, but Finn is harder. On hands and knees, I brace against the earth and wait for him to tilt my world off its axis. My panties are discarded and he bites each cheek, then trails his tongue up my spine. My eyes fall shut as he enters me on a rough stroke. I moan, loving the way he fills me, the way he grips my hips as he retreats, then pumps back in with a groan. My masquerade outfit is abandoned and I don't hold back. I'm finding out who I am. This is me, unashamed, begging him to go faster. Harder.

The sounds of our bodies slapping fill the night as we mate like wild animals. I can't call it lovemaking. Lovemaking doesn't really fit this raw urgency taking place. It's not tender or slow. He hits that special spot deep inside, and my orgasm builds, needing to be released.

"Ride me," he says, flipping us over, and pulling me on top of him. "Work your cunt all over me."

My rolling hips falter a moment at the word he used, but I'll decide later if I like it.

With apparent night-vision skills, Finn unhooks my bra and tosses it. "You have perfect tits." He cups my breasts. "I love the way they bounce."

As I circle and grind, seeking euphoria, he sits up, changing our position, and takes a nipple between his teeth. He's so bendy. And good with his mouth.

"Finn," I murmur. "That feels so good."

He rocks up into me, sucking and biting the sensitive peaks. I'm so close. Every cell tingles like a live current. And then I'm on my back, legs over his shoulders. I claw at the grass.

"Say my name again," he says, slamming into me.

"Finn."

"Louder."

"Finn."

"Scream my name."

"Finn," I yell. Hopefully, no wild animals are now curious what's going on in their territory. My orgasm fades, because now I feel silly. And I am not bendy. I drop a leg from his shoulder.

"God, you're so hot." In our scissor position, he scoots me along the grass with powerful pumps. I'm feeling like a lawnmower, but the climax will be worth it. "Your pussy is so fucking tight. So tight."

Although I appreciate the compliment, it's sort of distracting.

I give it back a little, to see how he likes it, "You're so big."

His hips buck faster. "You want my big dick?"

"Yes. So big." With each bounce, I continue, "So, so, so big."

My repetitive dialogue doesn't slow his pace. He loves it.

"You're so dirty. Tell me what you want me to do."

He adds a finger to the mix, pressing my clit, and my orgasm reappears.

"Yes, do that. Please, *please*, don't stop."

"You like it when I fuck your tight pussy?"

"Mm-hmm." Why is this a problem for me? Am I defective? I don't understand why I'm not preening with pride that he finds the lack of looseness sexy. Maybe it's the uncomfortable position with my leg askew and the course friction of the ground against my back. Well, if I don't say something, this was all for nothing and I could potentially have to fake my orgasm. I really don't want to do that. What lioness fakes it?

"I need on top."

"Ah, fuck yeah." We roll back over. "Ride my big cock."

That was easy. Ask and receive.

"Come for me, my little slut."

Ugh. I'm trying my best here. The odds should be in my favor. He's sexy and ripped and has a ginormous dick. So why am I struggling? This is taking way too long, but it seems rude to tell him I'm not feeling his dirty talk in the throes of passion. I'll just keep trying. I kiss him, long and slow, to avoid further talking. He leads me back to that rapturous place I was in before the jumble of Kama Sutra positions happened. Bubbles dance along my skin, ready to burst. Astride him, I plant my feet and use his solid chest for leverage to find reprieve.

Briefly, anyway.

I'm still sore from the workout yesterday, and my legs are numb from the numerous pretzel shapes.

This must be my punishment for trying to

distract from the Austin question with sex. I need to regroup, so I stop moving and attempt to clear my head. I'm hyper-aware of everything now and attaining climax seems impossible. I've been here before and don't want a repeat of all the things I've done wrong. Once you fake it, it becomes a cycle.

Finn bends up yet again, wrapping his arms around me. "Who do you belong to, Chloe?"

I can't answer. A shooting star streaks across the sky, and I wish...well, I can't say what I wish for in this moment. I close my eyes, and do something horrible, something shameful.

An owl hoots in the distance, repeating Finn's question, mocking me for imagining dark eyes and a dimple. Music notes lead me back to orgasm heaven, but I can't let myself unlock the gate. It's so wrong.

I open my eyes. Finn watches me, waiting for my answer.

If I say it, maybe it will make it true, "You."

I silently apologize and fake it.

TEN

RASPBERRY IS NOT MY COLOR. Turns out, all that scooting around on the lawn in the dead of night connected me with the wild in ways I couldn't have imagined—a spider bit me on the ass.

"You're so swollen, you remind me of a balloon," Austin says, peering over at my bloated face. "Bet that clown guy at the craft fair could shape you into a little animal."

"Please, don't make me laugh. If I split open, you'll never get history facts again." I claw at my neck and arms.

"Sorry," he says, but the humor in his eyes tells a different story.

"Thank you for taking me to the emergency room." Charlotte and Mr. Charlotte-to-be have an early meeting with their wedding planner later this morning and June can't see to drive at night, so Austin was my savior. "I hated to ask, but my body itches so badly, I didn't know if I could stay on the road."

"Don't be silly, Chloe. I didn't mind."

Why do these things happen to me? The spider bite is karma for the fauxgasm. When Finn drove me back to my place, I was so lost in guilty thoughts, I didn't pay attention to the faint itching of my body. Nor the soreness on my bottom. I wrote it off to an aftereffect from the spanking. It was my first time, so how was I to know the throbbing sensation stemmed from a spider?

After I showered, it was clear the red hue of my skin wasn't from the scorching water. Swollen and itching so badly I wanted to skin myself alive, I called Finn.

"Take some Benadryl, babydoll. You'll be fine," he said before he let me go so he could sleep.

Part of having a person is them being there for you in emergencies, isn't it? That article Charlotte wrote about superheroes was full of lies. SuperFinn did not rush to save me in my distress. Not to mention, I didn't even have Benadryl and therefore could have died. That's dramatic, but sue me. Not having to fend for yourself is an expected perk of a relationship I didn't receive. Well, at least I have friends to lean on at two a.m. when rogue spiders come calling.

Pink tinges the brightening sky as Austin pulls into the driveway and parks. "Do you need me to stay with you?"

"No, no." I grab my handbag. "The doctor said the shot will make the allergic reaction pass soon. Go home and get some sleep. That's what I'm going to do."

He bites his lip. "Is Finn coming over to stay with you?"

"No. He has a training session this morning, and after that, basketball with some friends." I see the judgement written all over his face. "It's okay, really. Thanks again." I open the door. "You're a lifesaver. Literally."

He pulls the key from the ignition. "I can't let you stay by yourself."

"I'll be okay."

Chivalry isn't dead. He ignores me and exits. Life would be so much easier if he'd drive away. How can I stop comparing the two men when Austin insists on staying and my boyfriend is nowhere to be found?

I'm too tired to convince him I'll be fine, so he follows me inside and I stretch out on the couch.

"You should go home," I tell him. "You must be exhausted too."

"Nope. Not leaving. I'll just take a nap."

I let my eyes drift close as he settles into the club chair angled across from me. Not exactly the nap date I wanted, but I'll take it.

I'M A FRAUD. A phony who skipped SuperFit to eat ice cream with Charlotte and Austin. It feels lovely to not suffer through leg lifts and grumble in my head the entire time, though. What a relief to take a day off from fitness. What a relief to just spend time with my people. Is it normal to have these thoughts only a month in? I'm sure it's not.

"You know, it just feels like I'm consumed by squatting and running nowhere on a treadmill," I say as we wait our turn at Every Day Is Sundae. "I don't get it. Am I supposed to get it? Is there something wrong with me?"

This is a question I truly need answered. It's been a week since the tiny house incident, and during that week, there's been no more sex.

"There's nothing wrong with you," Austin says.

"I think the amount of people here confirms ice

cream trumps exercise," Charlotte adds. "There's a delicate balance between healthy and fanatical."

The guilt weighing on my shoulders lightens. It's like a twisted form of aromatherapy, letting my troubles out, surrounded by the sweet scent of freshly baked waffle cones.

The line shuffles forward and so do we until it's reward time.

"What can I get for you?" the lanky cashier asks me.

Finn's lecture about making good choices blares in my mind.

"I'll just need a moment to decide."

While Austin and Charlotte order, the containers of frozen flavors behind the glass case tempt me to get a scoop of each. It's been weeks since I've indulged in decadent treats.

On the plus side, when I arrived, I could have sworn I saw Austin's eyes linger on my newly toned body. And Charlotte straight up smacked my ass and declared it hard enough to bounce a quarter, which caused Austin to involuntarily look a second time and make noncommittal noises.

On the negative side, if I still care that Austin's looking, and tallying the number of glances, then he definitely isn't out of my system.

Even though I desperately want the real thing, I say, "I'll have a scoop of fat-free vanilla."

"No, she won't," Austin says. He turns to me and lowers his voice, "You like chocolate peanut butter. Full fat. Full flavor. Fat-free is not you."

He's right. I faked an orgasm. Must I fake ice cream too?

"Give me two scoops of chocolate peanut butter, please."

"That's my girl," Austin says. "Today we're rebelling."

Yes. I'm not his girl, but I *am* a rebel. With our cups in hand, we head to the sprawling topping bar.

"Pain is weakness leaving the body!" Finn likes to yell at me in the gym. Clearly I haven't suffered enough, because I am weak enough to load a pound's worth of chocolate chips, peanut butter cups, and Oreos onto my double-scoop. No one judges me for my abundance of toppings, and it's nice.

With my weighted cup, I follow Austin and Charlotte to a vacant table.

"It feels so good to just relax today," Charlotte groans as she stretches across a whole side of the booth, forcing me to slide my supple rear just inches from Austin's. "My future in-laws are *a lot*. I thought wedding planning was exhausting on its own. And then slightly more so with my mother involved. But they are so picky you'd think it was their wedding. Or at least their money."

"I'm sorry," I tell her. "What are they giving you problems about?"

"Ugh, the venue for one." She points her spoon at me. "But this idea is the worst... They want a ring warming ceremony."

I laugh. "What's that?"

"His parents want our bands passed among the guests to lay their hands on. Margaret said it sends love and good energy to them." She shakes her head. "No. Just no. What if someone secretly sends bad vibes?"

"I think you're safe, even if they do," Austin says with a half-smile.

"Oh"—she turns to face us—"and this... Instead of bouquets, his mom said she could make wreaths. Wreaths."

"That's interesting," I say.

"No, it's not interesting. All I can picture is tossing my wreath instead of a bunch of flowers like I'm lasso-ing single bridesmaids. It's weird. I want the dream wedding with bushels of flowers. I want the whole fantasy. Ya know?"

Yeah, I do. Since Charlotte started planning her wedding, fantasies of my own have materialized. Her pending nuptials have unleashed a potential bridezilla within me. It's like women's menstrual cycles syncing. I've become matrimony synced.

"Isn't the dream ending up with the person you love?" Austin says, giving Charlotte a pointed look.

"No." She laughs. "Well, hypothetically, what would you guys want?"

Austin shifts on the red pleather and his forearm brushes mine. The innocent act causes the fine hairs on my arm to salute. Why must my body betray me in such cliché ways? I'm trying here.

"I don't know that I'll ever get married," he says.

"Really?" I can't help but ask.

His dark eyes stay on his strawberry ice cream. "It's not something I'm planning."

"What about you, Chloe?" Charlotte asks.

It's my turn to shift in my seat. "I don't know. I haven't really thought about it," I fib.

"Spill," Austin directs with a raised brow.

I dig tunnels in my ice cream with my spoon. "I guess for myself, I envision an intimate ceremony. The napkins will be printed with fun history facts of us. There'll be an artist live painting the ceremony so we can hang it in our home.

"Aw," Charlotte coos.

"Granny Mae will do the dessert bar, and the menu will be a replica of food from our first date." I look up. "Oh God, Finn and I had wings. I can't have messy wings in a white satin gown. I'll be starving at my own wedding."

Charlotte's spoon halts mid-air on the way to her mouth. "You'd marry Finn?"

"Well, no. I mean..." Warmth floods my face. "We're just dating." Awkward silence. "So, uh, how's the move going?"

"I'm almost all the way out," Charlotte says.

"What about you, Austin?" What I really need to know is, *have you found a roommate yet and please say Finn or a total hot babe hasn't signed up*, but that's not really something one blurts out.

"I'm still looking for someone else to rent the place," Austin adds.

Charlotte makes it so much worse with, "Isn't Lucy thinking of moving in?"

Somehow, I manage not to spin my head to Austin and continue with my mountain of ice cream as if his answer is meaningless to me. However, he doesn't respond. I move my gaze from whipped cream to him.

"Did you complete your menu yet?" he asks Charlotte. "You know I judge every wedding by the food."

She doesn't seem to notice he didn't answer her question and launches into a discussion about food options with Austin. But I notice. I notice everything.

If he isn't answering, he must be thinking about it. If Lucy is moving in, that means things are serious. But I guess that's the goal of relationships? It shouldn't be shocking they've moved to that stage, but it is.

A shadow darkens the table, and I look up to see a stern-faced Finn.

"Oh, hi," I say, much too bubbly. "Didn't expect to see you here."

"Thought you were trying out a new clay today."

"I did." Not really. "And rewarded myself."

His horrified eyes flit from the most likely fat-free sugar-free frozen yogurt in his hand to the mounds precariously balanced atop my full-fat, all-the-sugar ice cream.

"This"—he shows his sparse little cup with a frown—"is my reward for hitting a new personal record today. My reward for a solid workout. Which you were supposed to be joining me on."

"Oh, was that today?" I say, as weakly as my willpower. "I decided to get dessert at the last minute." Which is true, but if I'd been honest about my aversion to excessive fitness, maybe I wouldn't be in this awkward position?

"No dessert for deserters," Finn teases. At least, I think he's teasing. "Oh, hey, Austin," he says as if he just noticed who was at the table with me. "I've been meaning to ask if you want to shoot some hoops with me and a few friends?"

"I'll let you know."

They chitchat idly for a few minutes about basketball, and then I walk outside with Finn.

"Sorry about missing the gym." I should confess why I didn't show. "I just—"

He cuts me off, "You can make it up to me by coming to dinner with me."

A bit relieved I don't have to have this conversation in the parking lot, I agree, "Okay."

"I'll pick you up at six." He kisses my forehead. "We'll talk later."

Yes, we'll have a serious talk. At dinner, I'll tell him all the things I want to say and everything will work out.

ELEVEN

INTERNET EXPERTS RECOMMEND WAITING, at minimum, three months to introduce family. Of all the rules, I'd say this is most critical to heed.

I knew I should have made Finn turn the car around when he released the news that dinner would be at his parents' home. How do you fail to mention something that important? After being blindsided, I was too nervous to discuss the excess exercise. While he blasted Beethoven, I spent the twenty-minute drive researching appropriate time frames and one month-ish is not within the recommendation.

Breaking this commandment has resulted in dire consequences, preventing me from being accepted into the family fold. Seems like Finn's parents are a fifty-fifty split on me, and I'm at a loss on what to do to salvage this connection. It's important to love your boyfriend's family. And they should love you. Or at least tolerate you.

At this moment, I can only hope the spider indeed bestowed superpowers on me and I'll shoot webs from my hands and swing out of here.

"Why don't you lift Chloe over your head," his dad, Phineas, says. "Show us how strong you are."

Finn chuckles beside me on the linen-clad sofa, and I swear he's contemplating it. "She's wearing a dress, Dad."

"That she is," Phineas murmurs.

As his cornflower blue eyes do a lazy track over me, I...I am appalled.

Since we arrived for dinner, Phineas has not stopped flirting with me. It's overt and unsettling. A lingering hand on my shoulder after pulling out my chair at dinner. Placing my napkin in my lap. Making a "That's what she said," comment when I remarked, "I've never seen one that big" regarding their chandelier.

None of my ex-boyfriend's fathers made me feel uncomfortable, and I'm doing my best to pretend it isn't happening. I'd rather endure the daggers being thrown my way from Finn's new-ish stepmother.

"So, you're an artist?" Jacqueline, hurling another

subliminal knife at me with her narrowed hazel eyes, asks.

I fend off her dagger with a timid smile, hoping I'll wear down her hostility with my sunny demeanor. "Yes. A potter, specifically."

"I have no idea what that is," she says from a throne-like chair in their museum of a living room.

Finn failed to mention his family's obvious wealth. My mouth literally dropped open when he pulled into the circular drive of the Tudor-style mansion. The opulent house is filled with pricey artwork and plush furnishings. Which begs the question—why is he trying to move in with Austin?

"I make pottery," I tell her.

She scoffs over her scotch tumbler as if I'm a peasant on the verge of being tossed out. "And you earn money doing that?"

"Well, not yet. But I have a full-time job at It's Clay Time. I teach pottery classes to kids."

Beneath the chandelier's sparkling lights, this fancy form of interrogation is not going well. Why doesn't she like me? I'm likeable. I work with children, dammit! This is all so bizarre. There's a chance she doesn't like me because I can't stop staring at her. It's impossible not to, though. First, in a chic white pantsuit against the regal scarlet upholstery, she looks like a badass queen. Second, and most important,

Jacqueline and Phineas look like older replicas of me and Finn. If I were to keep up with the exercise and somehow acquire gobs of money, it's as if I'm seeing an uncanny future reflection of myself.

I mean, Finn has to realize this. Ew. Does he? Is that why she's looking at me as if someone told her I stole all of her Gucci. To test the theory, I place my hand on Finn's thigh.

Double daggers. Oh my God. Surely not?

"And what do you do, Jacqueline?" I ask. Because, I know nothing about these people, other than what I've gleaned from being here in the last hour—they're as healthy as Finn based on the walnut salad for dinner with no dressing. Or, as Phineas called it, a "naked" salad.

"She looks pretty all day," Phineas says. "That's her job."

Instead of throwing her wine at him, she bats her long lashes and gives him a coy smile. "Thank you, honey."

Phineas rests his shoulder against the marble mantle. "Finn mentioned you work out at SuperFit. How do you like it?"

"It's good," I lie. "Finn is a great trainer."

"Glad to hear that. I own them." Wait, *what*?

"You own SuperFit?"

"Yep. Two hundred gyms across the country.

Finn will take over when I retire." He flexes his bicep. "That might be a while, though."

When I glance over at Finn, his hooded gaze gives nothing away. That's a big deal he didn't mention it. We've only worked out there a bazillion times.

"So, you're just kind of working there to be like an undercover boss?" I ask Finn.

"Something like that," he says. "Have to pay my dues."

Phineas pushes off the mantle. "Why don't we burn off that dinner? We have a bowling alley in the basement." He crosses to me and holds out his hand. "Let's have a tournament and see if you're a SuperFit girl, Chloe."

This feels like a challenge, of sorts. I really don't want to take his hand *or* be a SuperFit girl. But what choice do I have?

"Is bowling really going to show you what kind of girl I am?" I hesitate to even ask.

"Bowling requires strength and agility. It requires focus. It's both mental and physical. Playing the beautiful game will absolutely show us what kind of girl you are."

I can't wait to disappoint.

With my hand tucked in his arm, I'm led out of the living room and down a wide hallway full of framed pictures of the family at various stages of their life. A toothless Finn grins at me from atop a mountain peak as we pass, and I'd rather spend time here, studying the photos, but that's not going to happen.

At the end of the corridor, we stop at a set of double doors. Phineas pushes a button and they slide open.

"You have an elevator?"

"Had it installed last year. It's a real time saver."

Funny people who are so fitness-oriented didn't choose the stairs for the single flight down. But that's not my business. I free my hand and scoot next to Finn in the corner, trying to get some cover from Jacqueline's eyeball-stabbing as we descend.

After a few seconds, we step out into an enormous room with two bowling lanes at the edge of the glossy hardwoods. It's a totally professional setup, complete with flat screen monitors overhead to keep score and neon blue gutters. Plump leather seating flanks the area.

"Wow, this is amazing."

"Thank you," Phineas says, walking toward a wall of shoes. "What size are you? We keep one of every size on hand."

"Seven."

While we lace up, I try to come up with a reason

to get out of here. I just want to go home, because truly I don't need to burn off that salad. There was no dressing, for fuck's sake. These people are rich, you can't offer a girl some ranch?

Finn dispels my hopes of escaping. "Listen, we need to win." He squats in front of my chair. "Got me?"

"Um, okay? I'll try my best."

"No. No trying. We *need* to win this." He glances over his shoulder to where Jacqueline is sharpening her knives. "She's good. But you need to be better."

"Okay, well...I haven't bowled since eighth grade, so...." It's not like I'm in a league or something and keep my skills up to date. And why must everything be a competition?

"Ready?" Phineas calls.

Not at all, but lucky for me, I go last.

Jacqueline and her special diamond-encrusted bowling shoes make a strike on her first attempt. So does Phineas.

And Finn.

No pressure.

I select my ball, bring it up balanced in both hands, and focus on the pins. When bowling originated, Germans believed knocking down wooden shaped pins would pardon their sins. I'm not certain this crowd would appreciate that nugget of information, so I keep it to myself and hope for a strike so my indiscretions will be forgiven. Because karma is really kicking my ass with this torture.

As I shuffle forward on the slick floor and swing my arm back, Phineas says, "Yeah, let's see if you're a stroker."

His words ruin my aim, and I release...straight into the gutter.

"Fuck," Finn mutters.

"Sorry," I say, walking over to him. "Isn't it about having fun and not whether you win or lose?"

"No," he answers. "Only losers say that. We need to win."

I tilt my head, wondering why this is so important and resisting the urge to tell him to blame his father for my performance.

"Uh-oh," Jacqueline says, with faux concern. "Looks like someone isn't happy."

She looks very pleased by that. I'm no conspiracy theorist, but this is a very strange dynamic between her and Finn. I stand on tiptoes and give Finn a brush of my lips.

Whoosh. Daggers.

Unbelievable.

The game continues, with Finn mumbling curse words at my performance, until we finally lose.

"Good game," Phineas says. "Sorry, son."

"Yeah, me too," Finn drawls.

"We'll head upstairs and give you some privacy," Jacqueline says. "Take care, Chloe."

My brow pulls tighter than my vagina. "What's going on?" I ask Finn as they step into the elevator.

"Listen"—his warm hand slips down my arm—"it's not you...well, it kind of is...but it's not going to work out."

"What do you mean?"

Am I being dumped? After all that? He's dumping me?

"I thought you could be a SuperFit girl, Chloe. Someone by my side to be there for me like Jacqueline is for Dad. Someone who appreciates how rough it is to maintain a body like mine. Someone who lives and breathes fitness like my family does. But it's clear that will never happen."

Not as clear as it is to me. This breakup is so horrendous, I'm speechless as he continues, "It's a shame because you really loved my cock. Greedy girl." He licks his lips and phew, the action is no longer appealing to me. "I need someone who will rule the empire with me and love it. A winner. This was a family test, of sorts. That you failed. So"—dramatic pause—"I can't see you anymore," he whispers, as though he's afraid this news might break me.

Shocked, I do a slow blink. "Wait. If we'd won, you'd want to keep dating? Your parents knew about this?"

"Yes and yes. But we lost, Chloe. And the rules are rules."

Bless you, rules. "I understand."

"And I want you to know that I've decided not to move in with Austin, out of respect for you."

This just gets better and better. "Respect?"

"I know how hard it is to get over someone you see a lot, so I'm going to take the tiny house."

Is he really this narcissistic and egotistical? How could I have missed it? Why does my radar not work? I'm tempted to point out that breaking up with him is not the hardship that he is presenting it as. I'm more upset over losing the tiny house. But it's easier to just let him think I'm distraught, so I roll with it.

"Yes. I would be very hard-pressed to get over this if you were around all the time."

He frowns. "Now, I do expect to be around here and there. You don't get to keep Austin all to yourself in this breakup."

This is where I draw the line. "But...he's *my* friend. Of course, I get to keep him for myself."

"He reminds you of me. I understand." He sighs and whispers, "I'm really going to miss your tight pussy."

I nod in commiseration. "With all that exercise it will only get tighter, but it will be okay."

He blows a breath. "I use the gym every morning from six to eight, over the lunch hour, and again from five thirty to eight. Beyond those hours, feel free to keep working out at SuperFit."

I'm having a hard time processing what just happened, so I say, "Thanks."

"You're great, Chloe. You really are. Look where you started and where you are now. And your job is so damn hot." He shakes his head. "You just need to believe in yourself. You might surprise yourself one of these days."

Well, that would be lovely. Because then I wouldn't be standing here being the one who got dumped.

In a weird way, I appreciate he believes in me. Someday, maybe someone will believe in my art.

At least I'm comforted by the knowledge that I have plenty of ab pics on my phone for the Netflix and solo-chill nights ahead.

TWELVE

I DON'T CARE if it's for the best, getting dumped sucks. No matter how wrong they are for you, they realized you're worse. Is a confirmation of all your shortcomings necessary? Even if you acknowledge you have them, it burns hotter than a thousand hells that someone else noticed them too and found you lacking. No one wishes to be lacking. Ask the rock Finn gave me. Not once did I wish for that.

If you think about it, the dumper is basically saying your imperfections are insufferable. In my opinion, a rule should be instituted that breakups can't occur unless both parties dump at the same time. It's a heavy blow to my self-esteem that I wasn't good enough to hold on to someone I didn't even want to hold on to.

Because I deserve it, our unexpected breakup has

me backtracking to all of my past relationship failures to kick myself. For some reason, Finn ending things over a ridiculous bowling game caused a lot more introspection than the previous boyfriends who lasted far longer.

With age comes wisdom, they say, but I don't seem to get smarter.

What really got under my skin was the "Hope you're okay" text Finn sent today. As if I shouldn't be okay. As if I can't function and crawled under a blanket weeping, praying for his return. Not at all. His message put me in an awkward position I don't appreciate. If I ignored him, he'd possibly think I'm devastated beyond repair and seek me out to confirm I was indeed okay. But I didn't want to reply, so I deleted it. Now I'll seem bitter. It's a classic catch-22.

To be clear, I'm not angry with Finn. Perhaps envious that in a twisted way he has a precise ideal of what he requires in a woman. Good for him. My wants in a relationship are shifting and changing daily. At twenty, all I wanted was a dude who didn't wear cargo shorts. Ha. Now I just want a guy who appreciates me. What the outcome will be, I have no idea. And now I'm not okay, because again, being dumped sucks.

Thank God for great friends. I have dragged myself from my mope-fest to help Charlotte pack.

Well, to *watch* her pack. What can I say? In terms of emotional support, hanging out at Austin's half-barren house, lounging in a beanbag chair, is just what I need.

"You guys can never dump me," I say. "I won't allow it."

Since the sectional is now gone to its new home at Charlotte's, she stretches out by my feet. "Chloe, as if. You're stuck with us for life."

"Thank you. I wonder if he'll want his rock back? I never should have invited him to the craft fair."

"Don't let this keep you from putting yourself back out there," she says. "Finn was a spring fling."

I like that term. Sounds sordid and is an accurate description of our brief time together. Of the four seasons of love, our short-lived romance fit spring best. I forced myself out there and planted the seeds. Who cares if it didn't blossom because Finn killed it?

"He was a nut," Austin says, propping up my fragile self-esteem. "Who makes you bowl competitively against his stepmother to decide if it will work out?"

Despite my doldrums, I laugh, because to hear it spoken out loud is comical. "And I tried so hard... I'm not a bowler. I still can't believe he sent me home in an Uber. Or that I had to leave through the secret entrance to the basement. Could it be worse? Well, yeah, it could've been worse. King Henry had Anne Boleyn beheaded."

Austin points at me. "That right there. How can he give up history facts?"

Cringeworthy moment happening right now. "I actually never shared any with him."

"Seriously? Why?" he asks.

I shrug away my discomfort. "Just didn't seem to fit our dynamic."

"Can I ask you something?" Charlotte says. "I'm not judging, but why did you stick with him so long? He wasn't very accommodating to your needs. It was a lot of what he liked and what he wanted."

Obviously they saw what I ignored in Finn, but kept silent so I could figure it out on my own. We weren't compatible. If he hadn't dumped me, I wonder when I would have given up trying to make it work? Never, probably. My track record is horrendous. In all probability, I'm going to die on that hill alone. My marker will read, "Here lies Chloe...forever alone."

"The abs, I guess." Superficial but true. It's embarrassing to admit to myself—to admit to my friends—it felt good to have someone who looked like *that* interested in *me*. Sad, but again, true. "There's no sense in denying a lustful attraction drove the time I spent with Finn."

"Well, can't blame you there," Charlotte says. "It was the dopamine." She explains the science behind her logic and how our brains produce more levels of dopamine in the newness of spring. "It's fascinating. All the colors and smells trigger us to fall in love. Or in your case, lust."

"I'll just close my eyes and hold my breath the next time I go outside." I sink further into the beanbag chair. "Oh, well. Now I can eat food that isn't steamed tofu. I won't ever have a six-pack, not that one was imminent."

"You've never struck me as a gym bunny in disguise," Charlotte says tactfully. Hey, now.

"I'm going to take up yoga, though."

Hard to believe those words are coming out of my mouth but I do actually mean them. I've gone over the classic pros and cons associated with breakups, and as much as I despised it, working out has toned me. I don't want to give it up entirely. Plus, if I join a yoga class, it will help *me* be the bendy one in my next relationship. That is, if I pursue another one.

"Yes. We can do goat yoga," Charlotte says. "That looks fun. Cute baby goats crawl all over you. A girl I work with says it's a stress-free workout."

"I should get a baby goat. They like hills and I won't die alone."

Austin rises from his chair and heads into the kitchen. "Be glad you lost at bowling, Chloe. Sounds like Jacqueline would've murdered you eventually."

I know. I know. Even if our split was inevitable and for the better, it still stings to be on the receiving end yet again.

"You know, I've never been the one to break things off." Just once, why can't I be the kind of girl who realizes this shit first and does the breaking up instead of the other way around? I should've ended it. There were none of the things I wanted: napping, cuddling, hand-holding. Finn never even slept over at my house. And now, I want to wallow in my despair. Not over losing Finn, over the fact I can't seem to find someone who is right. "I'm a terrible girlfriend. Clearly, I'm flawed."

"No, you're not," Charlotte chastises, rejecting my criticism with a shake of her head.

"You have to say that because you're my friend. Most likely, I would've ended up going to the Clown Motel to please him." I give her a pointed look. "Think about that."

"Hell no. I would've stopped you," she says.

"Would you have been able to? I'm sure I would've made excuses to go and been terrified the entire time."

"From a psychological perspective, until you

value things *you* want in a relationship, you're going to drag out the process with guys who are wrong for you."

"What does that mean?"

"Well, you're too focused on making the wrong people right. If you need to work that hard at something, it's time to quit."

"It's that darn masquerade outfit I never took off. I was masquerading all over the place."

Austin returns with a bag of chips. "Um...were you role-playing?"

It's probably my depressed imagination that he looks intrigued? "No. I read a column that said show who you really are and don't disguise yourself. And I planned on doing that, but trying to make myself enjoy his hobbies distracted me."

"Silver lining. That's great introspection. You're learning," Charlotte says. "But listen, I only know what I read or study. There's a world of difference in living it. Somehow, I lucked out and found my person early on. If I was single, I'd have gone for SuperFinn too."

"Adulting is hard," I whine. "I'm already a quarter into another year of my life. I'll be thirty before you know it. What if I'm still in the same spot at thirty as I am now?"

At this point, I don't even care that Austin is

witnessing my emotional breakdown. If I'm not sad, then it's like I wasted my time with Finn. In one of my searches, I read an article that stated the average age to meet your life partner is twenty-five. I've passed that milestone. So now what?

With patience, they listen as I lament about my many faults as a girlfriend—

1. I lied about what I like, subconsciously setting myself up for failure.
2. I'm selfish and salad-dressing shamed them in my head, instead of appreciating the meal.
3. I secretly hoped Jacqueline would slip and fall into the gutter in her bougie shoes.
4. I'm jealous of his tiny house.

They listen as I continue to lament about my weaknesses as a woman—

1. I'm slacking on my career plans.
2. I overanalyze things.
3. I'm slightly neurotic.
4. Can't keep a boyfriend because of aforementioned flaws.

It's a vicious cycle of doomed relationships caused by yours truly.

Of course my friends reject all my criticism. "You are SuperPerfect," Charlotte tells me. "Just the way you are."

There's no point in continuing to wallow; I don't miss him or want him back. And I've tortured them enough for one day, so I change the subject. "Did you find a roommate?" I ask Austin.

"Not yet." He grins. "Finn fell through."

I smile. "Sorry about that. He was a tad obsessed with you." As am I. But, I realize, less than before Finn came along. Huh. Well, that makes the Finn fiasco a tad easier to endure. As Granny Mae likes to say, "Look hard enough and you'll always find something to appreciate in the shit life hands you." With that in mind, I shovel through the poo and find more good. I relinquished the fear of dating and put myself out there. That accomplishment deserves applause. My inhibitions took a hike, and I tried new things, like wall sex and spanking outdoors. I toured a tiny house. See, I've grown from this experience in ways that aren't all bad.

Hopefully. Time will tell.

Like I said, my track record is pitiful.

As Charlotte and Austin discuss her move-out date, it hits me—how will this work?

I won't be hanging out here anymore without Charlotte living here. I hadn't really considered that part of Charlotte's new life. I'm sure we'll all get together, attend craft fairs and whatnot, but I won't just drop by after work. Austin is my good friend, but not my best friend. What's the etiquette if Charlotte's not here? Change isn't easy for me, and this is monumental.

More depressed than before, I scan the rooms. The cool kitchen full of Austin's cooking gadgets where we've laughed and had too many meals to count. The oversized living room with cathedral ceilings that hold secrets confessed over wine. The tall windows that showcase a view of the mountains. The cute blue door with a quacking doorbell.

"So no Lucy moving in?" Charlotte asks while I deal with my panic.

"No." Once again, he doesn't elaborate. "I'll probably run an ad, unless you know someone."

"Yeah, hm, I don't," Charlotte says. "How about you, Chloe? Know anyone?"

I tear my gaze from the light in the corner that would make an excellent spot for doing pottery, and impulsively volunteer, "Me."

SUMMER REBOUND

EPISODE 2

Summer is for throwing caution to the wind, and Dune's a bad boy that lives for danger.

Colorado is heating up, much like my newly re-discovered libido, and I'm hoping like hell that my new blind date's hot, too. Fate (and my bestie) truly deliver a doozy:

He rides motorcycles.
His tattoos are insanely hot.
The mystery of his life is all but unsolvable.

This good girl is about to get a little bit bolder in search of truth, justice, and a rebellious phase.

ONE

I'M ninety-nine percent certain my blind date belongs to a one-percent motorcycle gang.

Near a row of Harleys, I text Charlotte. **You failed to mention this is an actual biker bar.**

Oopsie daisy! she replies within seconds.

Srsly?

In my defense, isn't the name Handle Bar obvious?

Not really. Handlebar is also a kind of mustache.

How many mustache bars have you ever seen?

She has a point, but this is Boulder, so I can't rule

anything out. Still... **Not to be judgmental, but is this safe?**

Until now, letting Charlotte play Cyrano de Bergerac and use my FriendsOfFriends account to select a guy seemed like a brilliant idea. Since I seem to pick duds, why not let the person getting married choose? Now, showing up to meet a stranger, armed with only a name, seems foolish.

That's very judgmental, but yes.

A flurry of texts reminds me of why I agreed to do this.

In a crazy small world, Dune knows my cousin, Ben, in Seattle, whom she vetted him with.

It's been two months since the Finn fiasco, and more than ample time to pursue a rebound.

I've decided to be more daring this summer, and meeting someone sight unseen is for sure daring.

You can't back out, she finishes. **Walk in like the lioness you are.**

Honkey tonk music filters from the sprawling wooden saloon, and if anything, I want to promenade, not rawr. But I'm already here, so I'll follow through, because I can't wait to see who Charlotte has picked for me.

Okay. Going in. I'll let you know how it goes.

Just remember... You're trying new things.

My sanity is questionable, but I drop my phone into my handbag and forge ahead.

"Are you lost?" a gruff voice asks as I take baby steps toward the building.

I glance over to a strapping man with a beard to rival Santa's.

"No, I'm supposed to be here." The furrow between his bushy brow says he doesn't believe me, so I elaborate, "I'm meeting someone inside."

"Who?"

Even if it's not wise, the authoritative tone of his voice compels me to answer, "Dune."

"Ah. Follow me." His tree trunk legs power forward to the wide door.

"It's okay," I say to his leather-vested back. "I can find him on my own."

"Don't be shy, girl," he says. "We're all family here."

When he swings open the glass door, I step into a fantastical alternative world made of leather. As we amble into the rowdy crowd, it's painfully obvious why he thought I was lost. In my sundress and wedges, I might as well have *outsider* written on my forehead. It wouldn't be the weirdest thing here. A multitude of biker people gawk at me with unbridled curiosity as I follow my guide across the hardwoods. His beefy frame barrels through the patrons, until we stop a few feet away from a dark-haired man. "That's him at the end of the bar."

"Thank you. I didn't catch your name..."

"Call me Hambone."

Never in my life have I called anyone Hambone, but I do now. "Thank you, Hambone."

With a nod, he drifts into the melee mingling nearby and I shake off the urge to bolt when mystery man stands. All the blind date advice I read said to smile a lot, but that's impossible when your jaw is on the floor. Charlotte straight up chose the bad boy. That old three-second rule to determine attraction is a non-issue. A millisecond is all I need. Full sleeves of vibrant ink cover his arms from wrist to the edge of his white T-shirt, and anyone who thinks tattoos aren't sexy can never be my friend.

"Chloe, I'm Dune." His black boots stop in front of me. "Nice to meet you."

"Nice to meet you too." I've only seen one episode, but Dune looks like he leapt out of *Sons of Anarchy* right into this bar. And I am...living for it. Full on reveling in the way his tongue peeks out to make love with the lip ring in the corner of his mouth. I've never gone for a bad boy before, but hey, it's summer, and I'm learning to be brave.

With a hand on my lower back, he guides me over to his previous spot at the end of the bar.

"Frog, I need that stool," Dune says to a guy popping peanuts in his mouth, like he's catching flies. With fascination, I watch Frog all but leap from said stool.

"Is this your old lady?" he croaks out.

Biker or not, it's not nice of Mr. Absurdly Long Legged Man to call me an old lady. Way to make me focus on the fact I'll be graying in five years. Of course I don't say those things, because I value my rapidly aging life, so I wait for Dune to defend my honor.

"Not yet," Dune says with a thick-lashed wink.

"I'm only twenty-six."

Frog chortles. "An old lady is someone you're committed to. Girlfriend. Wife. Off-limits."

"Oh. Awkward," I joke.

Dune said "not yet," so that must mean he's attracted to me as well?

"You'll learn all the rules," Frog says before clasping Dune on the shoulder and leaving us alone.

Disappointed there are rules, I slip onto his vacated seat. As someone who is still googling dating rules, adding another set seems downright impossible.

"What would you like to drink?" Dune asks.

Wine would get me laughed out of here, I'm sure. "Beer is good."

In an amazing display of alpha, he looks over his shoulder at the bartender and telepathically orders by holding up two fingers.

"So you're a potter?" He straddles the stool, facing me, and reaches in to scoot my seat closer, leaving my knee a centimeter from his package.

"Yes."

"You don't strike me as a weeder. You seem too wholesome."

Hm. Wholesome isn't the vibe I was hoping to radiate, but more importantly, "Weeder?" The bartender slides two bottles toward us as I try to figure out if he means what I think he means.

Narrator: *he does, in fact, think being a potter means I grow cannabis.*

"Oh gosh, no. I make pottery."

"No shit? That's cute," he says. "My friends will be disappointed, though."

"Good thing family has to accept you anyway," I say, shocked I'm not darting out of here.

In fact, I'm more shocked at the intensity of my attraction. It's the tattoos.

"So"—he takes a long pull—"what made you use a dating app?"

Directness is an admirable quality, even if it

causes me to squirm in my seat. Perhaps if I took his approach, I'd have better luck and avoid things like bowling myself into a breakup. Here goes nothing.

He listens as I explain myself by blaming Charlotte, and then I confess, "She picked you, and we agreed to keep you a mystery until tonight."

He takes it in stride and explains how he ended up on the site. "My buddies forced me into it too." Dark eyes ravage my face. "Glad they did."

I guzzle my beer for courage. "If you don't mind, I have a few questions for you."

"Ask away," he says.

"Let me just get my list." Thanks to internet expert Henry—and the Finn fiasco—this time, I'm discarding the masquerade outfit and making sure what I want is front and center.

"You have a list?"

"Yes. Just a few need-to-know things." I pull out my paper and unfold it. "I know it might seem strange but—"

He slams his bottle down on the bar with a jolt and reaches into his vest. Oh God, I'm going to lose my life over wanting to know if he naps. "I. Love. Lists," he breathes out, emphasizing each word. "This is my list for today." My shoulders relax when he produces, not a switchblade, but a scrap of paper between his thumb and forefinger. "Shit To Do

Before Five o'clock." He leans closer and looks at me as if he might eat me alive. "I fucking list everything. What's your title?"

"Top Ten Important Questions," I make up on the fly, because there is no title. This is so not good, and I'm sure Henry is judging me. Not only is there no title, I only have five things on here. I'm not a die-hard list maker. I'm a jotter. More often than not, I arrive at the store and realize I forgot my list. The raw intensity in his eyes stops me from disclosing that information.

"Love it," he says. "What's number three?"

The lies continue, "Occupation?"

"I have a better idea," he says. "Let's guess. Limit of three answers."

"Oh, okay. Fun." I go for the obvious. "You own a tattoo shop?"

"Accountant," he reveals.

Wow. He's edgy-looking but can pay the bills on time. Truly, the perfect kind of bad boy. Damn, I'm a good dater. I never, *ever* would have guessed that he's a dang accountant, so good thing he set a limit on three wrong answers. Even if he only gave me one. But who's counting? Not the accountant.

"Wait..." A foggy memory of setting up my account materializes. "You're Hunter?"

"That's my legal name. Dune is my biker handle. Everyone calls me Dune."

"Ah. What's a biker handle?"

Enthralled, I sip my beer while he explains the process of unique biker nicknames that tell a story about the person.

"So what's your story?" I ask, chin in hand.

"Dune is a hill, and I like to ride my bike in the hills," isn't the cool story I expected, but I'm too taken aback by our hill connection to care. Our meeting must be fate. Maybe I won't die on that hill alone after all.

Before I can proceed with my list, the bartender announces, "Five minutes to Jell-O wrestling. Get your drinks now."

The crowd cheers, and I spy a group of various-sized women in one-piece black swimsuits, assembling near what looks to be a blow-up pool in the corner. If you've never witnessed Jell-O wrestling, I recommend you do so ASAFP. It's utterly fascinating watching the slip and slide until they declare a winner.

"Well, that's interesting," I say.

Dune chuckles. "Every Friday night is a different event."

"You should try it," the bartender suggests. "Round two is coming up."

"Oh, I couldn't." Could I?

"We have about three minutes to list why you can," Dune says. "Let me borrow your pen, Bill."

On a napkin he writes...

Reasons To Fucking Do It:

1. Why the fuck not?
2. Free drinks for a year
3. See number one.

"Wow. A year?"

Dune nods. "Let's say you come here once a week and drink three drinks. That's one hundred and fifty-six drinks multiplied by four dollars on average. That's over six hundred dollars you'd save."

Even if he mistakenly thinks I'm going to become a regular of the well specials, the mathematical statistics floating by his lip ring are the hottest thing I've ever heard. Hot enough to have me say something absurd. "Where do I sign up?"

"You sure?" he asks. "You don't have to do it."

"I'm trying new things," I tell him.

Ten minutes later, I'm suited up and standing in line to Jell-O wrestle. So what if I didn't follow Henry's dating advice? What if this is who I am? A Jell-O wrestling liar.

A slew of bikers crowd the area, and I've never

been more thankful for working out with Finn as Dune's dark eyes wander over my body. The ref sticks his hand in a bowl and fishes out my name to go first.

"I'm going to kick your little ass," my opponent, a silver-haired woman, threatens as I dip my toes into the squishy neon blue Jell-O.

"That's not very family-like," I whisper and proceed to set a world record for trying to back out.

And also for losing.

All I do is turn to the referee, swiftly losing my balance, and the wild woman takes that as a signal to lurch and drown me in Jell-O.

"You lasted three seconds," Dune says, helping me from the pool. "Three is my favorite number. It's fate."

Maybe it is. You lose some. You win some.

TWO

APPROVED Qualities Of A Bad Boy:

1. Tattoos
2. Gives cheater who defeated you a
   withering death stare
3. Tattoos

ONE THING I didn't consider when signing up for
this humiliation—Jell-O hair.

After changing back into my clothes in the bar's
spacious and pristine bathroom, I towel off as much
goo as I can.

"So you and Dune are dating?" a woman in
leather chaps and a rhinestone flag bra asks.

"We just met tonight," I explain. "I'm Chloe."

"Hope," she says.

"Is that your actual name or biker name?"

She laughs. "Both. This is your first time here?"

"Did my faux leather bag give it away?"

"I was once in your place. Let me give you a few tips." She perches on the counter. "Don't touch his vest. Stay classy and get along with the other ol' ladies, and you'll do just fine."

I'm not sure how classy and Jell-O wrestling can ever go hand in hand, but I smile anyway and try to absorb as many of her helpful hints as possible.

Sounds like if I reach girlfriend status, I'm golden within their tribe. It also sounds like I will never reach that status because there are a billionty rules.

"I really appreciate your knowledge," I say, dropping the towel into the designated hamper.

"Any time." She hops down and walks out with me. "Looking forward to seeing you again. If not, love your shoes."

"Love your sparkle," I say before she's whisked away by a bald buff guy.

Dune approaches with a frown. "I have an emergency," he says.

"What's wrong?"

"Coco is sick."

There's no time to inquire who Coco is, because

he tells me he has to cut our date short and drive me home.

"Oh, okay. I understand. I'll call an Uber."

"No. I'll take you."

He ushers me at a rapid clip out of the bar to a black and chrome Harley. It's a beautiful yet masculine machine, but something I'd prefer to admire from afar.

"Go to Coco. I'll just—"

He swipes a black helmet dangling from a nearby handlebar. "Wear this. We need to get going."

It seems imperative I not waste time and balk at the stolen helmet, so I slip it on. "Good girl," he says, climbing onto the leather seat and patting behind him.

God, he looks hot sitting on a motorcycle. Bet that half-helmet doesn't even dream of giving him helmet hair. I can't believe this is *my* date.

He pats again. "Climb on."

There's no discreet way to do this in a dress, so I put my modesty aside and settle behind him. It's comfy. And intimate. There's nothing to hold on to except his hips. Not that I'm complaining. I give him my address, and like a clap of thunder, his bike rumbles to life. Bummer no one is out here to see how cool I must look. However, there are about a thousand vehicles who see just how uncool I look as he races down the road, making low to the ground hairpin turns. Yeah right, don't touch the vest. I'd like to see someone try to pry my death grip from it as I cling to him, with eyes squeezed shut, waiting to crash at any moment.

"Thank you, Jesus," I whisper when we finally arrive home in one piece.

Dune climbs off and removes my helmet. "I want to see you again," he says, eye-fucking me. "Next Saturday."

"Okay," I say, breathless. Even if I thought I was going to die on the ride home, being on a motorcycle was an unexpected form of foreplay. Every cell hums as if I just took a ride on a giant vibrator. My confused body wants to kiss the ground, thankful I'm alive, but also hump it.

Like a gentleman biker, he offers his hand to assist me off the bike. "I'm going to take you rock-climbing. It's fitting."

"How so?" Am I the only person who is happy with a movie and meal?

"Because you gave me a rock. Well, your friend did. Now I need to give you one back."

Damn you, FriendsOfFriends Marketing Department. The earnest look on his rugged face prevents me from dashing his plans. One physical date won't kill me, and I'll be vocal if I hate it. Plus, there's a possibility he'll take his shirt off and I can discover if other ink treasures exist.

"That's sweet. Sounds exciting."

We exchange phone numbers and my heart races faster than he drove here when he runs the pad of his thumb along my bottom lip.

"It's going to be hard"—he blows out a breath—"but I can't kiss you until the third date."

Internal sigh.

He's not a guy who seems like he waits for anything, so I can't help but ask, "Why?"

"Because I like you. So I need to do it when it's my favorite number."

"Got you," I manage to say.

If swooning existed, I'd swoon right here in the driveway. He's so sexy in the moonlight with his tousled hair and inked arms. Like I'd date his arms, if I could.

Somehow, he slides a hand into my matted hair and hunches down to take a deep inhale. "You smell like strawberries."

"It's the Jell-O," I whisper.

"Mm." He releases me with a pained groan. "You're too tempting. I should go."

I'm not opposed to that when the porch light flickers on, casting a spotlight on our hidden moment. The light goes off, but I can't shake the feeling Austin is lurking at the window like a parent.

"Okay. Thanks for the ride home."

"A man never lets his date leave in an Uber."

Take that, Finn. Condors soar in my belly as he slings a leg over his bike and revs the engine. Have I finally found a real man?

As Dune's bike roars away, Austin sticks his head out. "He's leaving so soon?"

I brush past him and his questioning look at my stiff, Jell-O head. "How very dare you, sir? I am a staunch third-dater. Don't ask about my hair."

"I had already decided I might not want to know what was happening there."

"Well, good." Things have been a little tense between us. We've already had a couple of roommate altercations, because you never really know someone until you live with them. Turns out living with a chef comes with a few unspoken rules of which I was unaware. For example, there's only one way to load a dishwasher, and even if the cycle is halfway through, one must stop the cleansing in order to redo the arrangement inside. Or that "kitchen shears" have a different meaning for someone who spatchcocks their own chickens for roasting, and one may not utilize them to trim one's bangs. Not to mention, pans are stacked by coating and not size. I can only assume moving the Jell-O from my hair into a bowl for midnight snacking is frowned upon for similar reasons.

"Is there food that isn't Jell-O?"

"Nothing special. Didn't you literally just get home from dinner? What kind of date doesn't feed you?"

"First date *drinks*. I'll just make a sandwich."

"Hey, Chloe," Lucy says from the couch, glamorous as always with shimmering hair. "Austin was so cute. Like a big brother waiting for his little sister."

Well, don't I feel incestuous. Showering should be first on the agenda, but now I need to eat my feelings.

"I'm a big girl. No need to worry about me," I throw over my shoulder on my way to the kitchen. In honor of my new friend Hambone, I grab capicola from the alphabetically arranged deli drawer.

While I slather mustard on the bread, a shadow falls across the counter. I look up to see Austin propped against the arched entranceway, arms crossed.

"I don't even pretend to understa—" He looks at my half-made sandwich. "What are you doing? What is that?"

He seems alarmed by my French's squeeze-bottle and packet of individually wrapped cheese slices.

With pinched lips, he stalks across, swipes my sandwich, and drops it into the trash. "Austin, what are you doing?"

"You're relieved of kitchen duty. Have a seat while I show you what a real sandwich is."

"Tell me all about your guy," Lucy says, joining the ambush. "If he works out at SuperFit, I might know him."

As I settle at the breakfast table with Lucy, Austin gathers everything to build new and improved sandwiches. The kind with ripe tomatoes. Lettuce that doesn't come shrink-wrapped in a big, tasteless ball. He makes bacon and not in the microwave. This is *living*. And to think, SuperFinn thought he would swoop in and take this away from me. Nope, don't think about your ex, after a date, in front of your roommate crush. Former crush. Former-ish. The crush has faded exponentially since I moved in with Austin. It's minuscule. As long as I don't look at his arms rippling as he chops. Or how he all but dances around the kitchen so gracefully. Or the way his gray pajama pants cling to his hips.

"Yeah, how did the blind date go?" Austin asks, flipping strips of sizzling bacon.

"It was..." I pause to select the right word. I've banished *good* from my vocabulary.

"If you take that long to think about it, it wasn't great," he says.

"Yes, it was." Sure, the Jell-O thing wasn't fantastic, and I accomplished nothing I set out to do, but there's insane chemistry and date two is my opportunity to correct my mistakes.

"Mm-hmm." He looks over his shoulder at me.

"You don't seem the biker type," Lucy adds.

"I'm learning I don't have a type." And I like that new discovery about me. "Plus, I'm expanding my horizons."

"Is he in a motorcycle club?" she asks.

"I don't know?"

"Did he have patches?"

Clearly, I failed at this date. If his sexiness hadn't consumed me, I would have noticed that detail. "I was busy Jell-O wrestling, so things kind of slipped by me."

In slow motion, Austin turns around. "I don't... Did I hear that correctly? Jell-O wrestling?"

"Is it really so shocking?" I could bring up the handcuffs I found in his room, but I won't.

"Well yeah, it kind of is," Lucy says, with wonder-filled eyes. "But opposites do attract."

"We're not that different," I say. "Are we?"

"Polar. He's a biker," she says. "You rarely go out. You're...you're a homebody." She places her hand on mine. "Not that staying at home is bad. I worked with a girl once who people nicknamed Boring Belinda. Sounds mean, but God, she really was boring. Like prop your eyelids open with toothpicks boring. Once, I dozed off in a meeting when she presented a new campaign. Anyway, the point of the story. As boring as she was, she ended up married to a guy in a rock band. Maybe this guy is *your* rockstar. See?"

Um, no, I don't see. Is she implying I'm boring? If she wasn't so nice, I'd find it offensive. Am I boring? Lucy would have thrown her hands in the air and squealed with glee as Dune rocketed across town at ninety miles an hour. She would never put nap dates on a list, which is why she gets nap dates. Oh God, I'm boring. I'm never going to get my bad boy kiss once he realizes I'm Comatose Chloe. Charlotte inadvertently teased me with something I really want, but will never attain.

"Hold one moment, please." I scoot away from the table and zip across the tiled floor. "I'll be right back."

Dull people don't do what I'm about to do. I fish my phone out of my bag and type out a message to Dune.

"Maybe you should pick me up at three o'clock since it's your favorite number?"

Okay, maybe they do. That was lame. I'll think of something better after I eat.

"So are you seeing him again?" Lucy asks when I return.

"Yes. Next Saturday, he's taking me rock climbing." Austin's judgies are palpable as he pats the bacon with a paper towel so I say, "Look, he's a respectable accountant, not a criminal."

"You had no idea Finn was a millionaire in training with a stepmother fetish, so yeah"—he lifts a brow—"your endorsement is weak."

"It's not like I can just ask him if he's in a gang." How does one address that without being offensive?

"I can ask him," he says.

"Oh my God, no."

He finally drops it to focus on finding the crispest leaves of lettuce with the perfect crinkle edges. Forty minutes later, when I gobble my gourmet sandwich, I wonder how it's possible that someone so *anal* can also be so hot. Perhaps, I should add it to my list of approved qualities.

THREE

THINGS I Never Realized Turned Me On:

1. Country music
2. Wallets on a chain
3. Spreadsheets

DUNE'S naughty lip ring all but begs me to make out with it while he rambles on about the importance of spreadsheets.

"If I ever get my business going, I'll use one to keep things organized," I promise as he drives through town to our rock date destination.

"Do it. It's a calculator come to life," he says with such passion, I want to live in a spreadsheet.

He's so intelligent and has shared all kinds of business advice this week in our text messages and calls.

"Just need to make a quick drop at the clubhouse," he says, turning down a tree-lined road.

Can't help but notice he said drop and not stop. My heart pounds and not the pitter-patter kind from staring at him. Is this Jeep filled with drugs?

"What are you dropping off?" I ask, casually.

"The helmet from last week."

Ah, phew. All week Austin has planted doubts in my mind that Dune is nefarious. I'll be happy to report my bad boy is a good boy.

He stops at a gate bearing two skulls with snakes slithering in their eye sockets. "Let me in," he says to the intercom.

"What's the magic word?" a female voice asks.

Nice. Equal opportunity employers.

He huffs and then says, "Please."

I smile as whoever is on the other side swings open the gate and allows us access to a sprawling area of land. It's not the warehouse-style clubhouse I expected to see. At the end of the drive sits a massive two-story log house with a wide front porch. Okay, I can handle this.

"This is beautiful. It looks like somewhere I'd

want to sit and sip hot chocolate by the fire on a snowy day."

Dune grins. "It's the Pres's house."

Ah, they have a president. While that hierarchy sinks in, he parks by a cluster of motorcycles.

"It's picnic day. Let's grab something to eat before we head out."

Um, picnicking is not a quick drop. Why must everyone spring things upon me at the last minute? Someone needs to put that in the dating rule hand-book, because *none* of my extensive research says to blindside your date with meeting new people. Not to mention, we brought nothing to the picnic. Granny Mae always says to never come empty-handed.

"Well, we didn't bring any food."

"No one cares," he says, retrieving the helmet off the back seat.

Sure they don't. They may say that, but if this relationship continues, I'll be nicknamed something horrible like Freeload. "Is there a nearby market?"

He grins. "You're adorable. But they really don't care."

In my biker etiquette research, I learned that challenging your man is frowned upon, and... I already know that's something I'll never follow.

"She cares." I point to a passing woman in jean shorts with an armload of Tupperware.

"Maggie," he calls out to her.

She waves and pivots. "Hey, Dune."

"Can you come here for a second?" She nods and sashays up to the Jeep. "My girl refuses to go in without food. Says it's rude. Can you spare something?"

Gasp. His girl. The fact he ratted me out is forgiven immediately under the terms of the Bad Boy Law of the Universe.

"Sure." She hands him a square container. "Take these cookies."

"That's so nice of you," I say, awed by her generosity. "Thank you. I'll pay for them."

"No, no. Girl, we're good. Don't mention it," she says. "See you out back."

"Happy now?" he asks when she's gone.

"Very. That was sweet of her."

With my borrowed cookies, we head to a manicured backyard laden with beards, red gingham tablecloths, and an assortment of food. Anything you could want—burgers, hot dogs, ribs, potato and pasta salads, grilled chicken, on and on. All things that would work as a first date wedding dinner. Not that I'm even thinking of getting married, but anywho. No one seems to mind our sporty attire, possibly because Dune has accessorized his black athletic shorts and Harley T-shirt with a leather vest.

As he's greeted with hearty back slaps, I hang back a bit, soaking it all in until a stocky man with a bushy beard approaches.

"Who's this, Dune?" he asks.

"This is Chloe, Pres."

Pres holds out his hand for me to shake. "Hi, Chloe."

"Hi, Mr. President." Hearty laughter ensues. Everyone thinks this is so funny, but hello, I literally don't know his name.

He nods to my container. "What do you have there?"

"Cookies."

"Love cookies. What kind?"

That's an excellent question. Since I have no clue the answer, I improvise and remove the lid to reveal unidentifiable misshapen tan cookies the size of a quarter. Great.

"See if you can guess," I say.

He selects one, and suddenly many hands are everywhere grabbing a sample like I work at Costco. In order to complete the charade I baked these, I snag one too, so I know the answer. Like a weird cookie gang bang, we all take a bite. Oh, dear. My tastebuds revolt.

Not to be ungrateful to Maggie's selfless gift, but

it's so dry and bland I can't figure out what kind it is. Other than awful. Sorry, Maggie.

Mr. President chews slowly, with narrowed eyes, and I'm impressed at his ability to swallow the darn thing. "Sugar?" he says.

I nod, because at this point it doesn't matter. My cookie reputation is unrepairable. No one will ever trust anything I bring again. Somewhere, Granny Mae weeps.

Dune's humor-filled gaze meets mine. "Let's go put them on the table." He leads me away. "Your face was priceless. What the hell is that cookie?"

"That cookie is a lesson to never show up empty-handed," I say and sigh. "I'm a fraud and got what I deserve."

He steps in front of me to massage my slumped shoulders, kneading the sagging muscles. "They like you. Shitty cookie or not. Sometimes you gotta roll with it."

Seems I'm always rolling. I'm a tumbleweed, drifting who knows where. But that's what I do for the next half hour. I could list all the ways I'm rolling.

Ways I Roll:

1. When Jell-O Woman, aka Bev, asks if I
   want a rematch, I laugh and say, "You're

the champion and I respect that," even though she basically cheated.

2. When Frog says my cookie nearly choked him to death and to please never bring them again, I smile and tell him he'll catch more flies with honey.

3. When Dune disappears inside for a twenty-minute game of pool, I hang out by the deviled eggs and have an impromptu egg-eating contest with a man named Goose.

THAT'S HOW I ROLL. Whether they like me is questionable, but they're at least tolerating me, so that's good.

When we leave, I'm all ready for a brand new shiny gym with no Finn in sight, but Dune keeps on driving right out of town.

Puzzled, I ask, "Where's the gym?"

"Gyms are for pussies." He winks. "We're going to rock climb like *men*."

I peer down at my pink tank and black athletic shorts to confirm my breasts and vagina are still there. I was very nearly a SuperFit girl, now I have to be a man?

"Don't I need training for that? I mean, it's a mountain?"

"We're starting out easy with bouldering."

"That doesn't sound easy." I laugh, but I'm dead serious.

He chuckles. "You can trust me."

Hopefully, that's true. This explains why he picked me up in a Jeep instead of on the bike. Oh well, I'd be lying if I said I wasn't relieved we're not going to the gym. Although, I'm less relieved now considering my imminent death by fall, rather than by a crash.

The dating experts say to keep a positive mindset if you want a positive outcome, so I banish all negativity. I'm sure Lucy wouldn't think a thing about being thrust onto a real mountain. She'd jettison up using her shiny hair for rope. I can do that too. I'm going to be the most exciting climber that ever climbed. Those rocks won't know what to do with all my non-boring sass.

With the top down on the Jeep, my tornado hair provides cover to ogle Dune as he drives. A country music song about a good man blasts into the warm air, while I study the art on his arms. He's like a painting I want to deconstruct. Last week, in the bar, the dim lighting shadowed the intricacies of his tattoos.

I lean closer toward a robed figure sitting on a hill near his elbow. "Is that Jesus?"

"Yeah," he says. "Got that one a year ago."

Well, take that, Austin. He can't be in an illicit gang. What criminal would tattoo Jesus? That would be hypocritical, right?

"So, you're a religious man?"

"Nah," he says. "Thought it was cool because of the Holy Trinity. Three, ya know?"

I should just come out and ask like Austin suggested, but my research of bikers over the week doesn't recommend it.

"Would you ever get a tattoo?" he asks.

"A tattoo has never been on my to-do list, but who knows?" I hedge.

"I like your unmarked skin. But if you ever decide to get one, maybe I'll get another. It's addictive."

So are the lazy circles he's tracing on my thigh with his thumb.

He turns down a bone-jostling gravel road, and then parks in the shade of towering pines.

"We're just going to hike that trail to a creek bed and that's where the boulders are."

Lovely, a hike before the climb. Positive mental attitude, I remind myself. The aim is to make today successful, so I can move on to round three of kissing.

That sounds ridiculous. When did I become a walking hormone and not an intelligent woman achieving her life goals? Is this really my objective? He looks over at me and the sun glints off his silver lip ring. I'll work on my issues after date three.

"Ready when you are," Positive Me says.

"Let me grab the stuff."

We hop out and he bounds to the back of the Jeep while I survey the mountainous landscape.

"You're going to love this," he says, slinging a backpack over his shoulder.

"Hopefully," I say with a smile.

He does the most wonderful thing—he offers me his hand, palm up. According to statistics, this means you're deeply attracted to someone. Swoon.

SEEMS I lost my positive attitude somewhere between the uphill two-mile hike and quicksand riverbed. This blows. I was tired before we reached the boulders and now, watching him scale and stand astride a large rock, I'm exhausted.

And gassy. Like shifting these rocks into a new tectonic plate formation kind of gassy. Ugh. Why did I eat all those eggs? Seriously, could my dating capabilities be any worse? There's no way I'm getting up there and putting my butt in his face.

Luckily, I've learned the art of flattering appreciation can replace an awful lot of actual doing on my part.

"I think I want to watch you do it a few more times before I try," I call up to him, wishing it weren't so quiet here among the pines, so I could release some of this excess air from my body. "You're a master at this stuff."

He gives me a thumbs-up. It's truly impressive what he's doing. Kind of like games of pool at a biker picnic, I never realized how mathematical rock climbing is. But I failed high school geometry twice, and therefore neither activity is for me.

After conquering yet another boulder foe, he yells, "Rocks are a little tricky to grasp today. I think you should just watch."

"Fantastic idea. I enjoy watching."

One thing I learned from SuperExBoyfriend at least, was not to kill myself being someone I'm not, so I focus on the two things I am qualified for: putting chalk on my Boulder boulder-er's hands, and taking surreptitious pics of his ass for Charlotte.

FOUR

MY BAD BOY HAS A BOO-BOO. Blood oozes from Jesus, plopping a drop of scarlet onto the boulder by my feet, and I'm going to hell. I ask Tattoo Jesus to forgive my selfishness, because I should feel sorrier for Dune, but honestly, it gets me out of doing anything that could cause a far worse boo-boo.

"I think you might need stitches." A bunch of them.

"It's just a scratch," he says. "A flesh wound."

"It is *not* a flesh wound. This is some Black Knight Monty Python shit right here."

"I can't even feel it." The look on his face says otherwise.

"Well, I don't like seeing it." Woozy, I point to the ground. "Come down here."

"What's the magic word?"

"Please."

He smirks, but to my relief, obeys. "Now what?"

"I don't know," I murmur. "Hospital?"

"No way," he says. "You need to chill."

Jesus is weeping blood, and what I need is either a tourniquet, or an old priest and a young priest. Our dirt-stained shirts, from scooting around on boulders, are potential germ factories, so I reach inside my tank and sacrifice my bra. Ugh, it's my good one, but Jesus made far greater sacrifices than a fifty-dollar La Perla bra. "Want to see some real magic? Watch this." Like a magician, I unhook and slip the delicate fabric out of the armholes without having to remove my top.

"Ta-da." This isn't how I envisioned him seeing it when I put it on this morning, but a gaping wound trumps seduction.

"Damn," he says. "Virginal white. Girls think white is boring, but it's so fucking hot."

"Cover your ears, Jesus," I say as I wrap my bra around his arm. Hopefully Dune is too delirious to notice the padding that gave my breasts extra oomph.

Once it's secured, I'm impressed with my handiwork. "Hopefully the titty tourniquet stops the bleeding."

He laughs, and this is no time to laugh. "You're funny," he says.

What I am is scared...and still gassy. I could blow us back to the Jeep. TMI, I know.

"Let's go," I direct him.

Adrenaline powers my feet back to the miles-away vehicle.

"I'll drive," I say when we reach the Jeep. "Just in case you feel faint."

"I'm really okay," he says, but gets in on the passenger side and hands me the keys.

I peel out of the loose gravel as he sets the GPS on his phone to guide me.

"If you won't go to the emergency room, I'll take you to my place and bandage it. My roommate is a chef and has these special butterfly Band-Aids for when he slices himself. He says they're as good as stitches."

His pale face whips to me. "Your roommate is a guy?"

"Yeah. I just moved in a few months ago." There's an odd tension in the air that I feel the need to dispel. "He has a girlfriend."

"Ah, okay." He relaxes back against the seat and closes his eyes. Traffic is light and I make it to my house in under an hour. To my dismay, Austin and Lucy's cars are in the drive. Bright side, my gas is gone. There is always something to be thankful for, as Granny Mae says.

Dune follows me up the cobblestone path and inside where Austin and Lucy are nowhere to be seen. Probably napping together.

"Let's go to my room." I make a pit stop at the hallway bathroom to collect peroxide, cotton balls, and the special bandages, and hurry him to my bedroom before Lucy and Austin appear to make criminal accusations.

"Have a seat." I close the door.

"Cute room," he says, taking in the colorful pottery arranged on a shelf draped in twinkle lights behind the bed.

"We can tour later. Sit."

"You're sexy taking care of me," he says, plopping on the edge of the bed.

I toss my supplies beside him. "You're always sexy."

"Yeah?" He traces a finger along the hem of my shorts.

"So sexy," I whisper.

But this is not the time to flirt. He's bleeding to death. "Let me wash my hands." I disappear into the en-suite bathroom for a quick scrub and a toot and fly back. "Okay, your nurse is here and ready to mend you." I step between his spread legs. "Be a good patient."

"I see your nipples," he rasps. "You have great

tits. Full and bouncy." He palms them. "Are you a naughty nurse?"

"Yeah," someone that is *not* me screams out. "Oh, yeah. Yes. Yes. Yesssssssss."

Dune releases my breasts. No way. Rapid squeaking confirms what I hoped wasn't happening is happening.

Austin and Lucy are banging across the hall.

Horrified, my wide eyes lock with Dune's as I untie the blood-stained bra. "Looks like it stopped bleeding. Does it hurt?"

A husky groan assaults my ears, followed by a high-pitched squeal. "Yesss. Yesss. Ooo. Uh-huh. Yessss."

Weird doesn't describe that we can hear them, or that it seems Lucy is answering my questions, but I roll with it and dab at the drying blood with a perox-ide-soaked cotton ball.

"To answer your question, it doesn't hurt," Dune says.

"Good. I'm trying to be gentle." Unlike Austin, who is banging the headboard against the wall like he's trying to renovate the house.

This is the first experience I've had of their sex shenanigans since I moved in, and I don't like it. Explicit audio isn't a reality I was prepared to hear. I want to stuff these cotton balls in my ears. Logically,

I know it's taking place between them since they're a couple, but out of sight, out of mind. An image of a naked Austin, thrusting into Lucy, replaces the damage to Jesus I'm trying to repair. Judging by the increase of squeaking, he's thrusting like a maniac.

"I think a squeal is coming soon," says Dune.

On cue, Lucy yelps. I giggle. She lets out another yelp of pleasure and unwanted jealousy sparks.

With gentle fingers, I cover Jesus with an over-sized butterfly Band-Aid so he can't see the sinful fire of envy blazing throughout my body. "All done."

Dune fists the hem of my tank and tugs me toward him. Nose to nose, he says, "We've gotta go to my place next time."

"What would we do at your place?" I ask, hoping to instigate a one-upping contest by banging Dune.

"Not that." He flips me onto the bed and braces on his good arm. "He's doing it all wrong. You'd come much faster than she will."

"Well, that's a mighty big statement."

"So is this." He grinds into me and one-upping vanishes from my mind. "I need to kiss you."

"Then kiss me," I urge. Not under the best of circumstances, but I want it now. With the luck I've had so far, date three may never happen.

Anticipation is a gut-twisting emotion. Is he going to do it or not? Blood rushes in my ears, drowning out the sounds coming from across the hall. Briefly.

"Please," more porn star moans, "do it, you wild animal," Lucy yells amidst the creaks. "Do it." Long groan that borders on exaggerated. "Do itttttt."

"God, could he just do it already? Her dirty talk is fucking boring," Dune says, catapulting into keeper status.

"Back to that kiss," I remind him so I can forget what's happening in Austin's bedroom.

He wets his lips and hovers his mouth over mine before finally giving me a taste of his lip ring. Unf. It's a soul-searing kiss that erases my mind of anything except the way our tongues circle in a head-spinning tangle.

Within minutes, it escalates into no-turning-back territory when he tears his lips from mine to suck a path down my neck and across my collarbone. "I need to be inside you."

Date two was not the planned time for this. I don't even have the good undies on. But this is my authentic self, dammit, in mismatched cotton and lace. The internet gurus will disown and ban me from the inter webs for having sex so soon. There must be some caveat when it involves a bad boy. Everyone knows bad boys cause rash decisions and are irresistible. It's the law of the universe, therefore, excusable.

His fingers find their way inside my panties to tease my seam, while Lucy hoots and hollers about a sexy beast.

"Seriously, I couldn't handle that," he says, working me into a frenzy with his hand. "How is he okay with that?"

"You like dirty talk?"

"Oh, yeah." He rocks into me, hard and thick. "Why don't you give me some."

I'll do anything to drown out Lucy. I attempt it, although I'm not sure how, "Oh yeah, you like that big dude? Big boy," I say louder than necessary. That seemed pretty good. "Big boy! Do you like that, big boy?"

He halts his fingers. Oh God. He's not impressed.

"Yeah, um, my mom calls me that. You're going to have to stop that immediately."

His directness is goals.

I make another attempt. "Maybe I need a spreadsheet filled with dirty talk words." I'm onto something, because his dark eyes flare. "I'd make a column just for your cock."

"That's it, dirty girl. You'd need eight rows to fit

me." He groans, circling my clit. "Insert a column for your pussy."

I'm still processing the eight inches, but this is hotter than expected. Lucy's theatrics can't stop me.

"I'd add another column for how fast you make me come. A column full of numbers." I suck his earlobe into my mouth. "What do you think the first number will be?" He moans when I whisper, "Three?"

In a flash, Dune stands and removes my shorts. "Maximum three minutes to make you come." His chest rises and falls at a rapid pace, while he retrieves a condom from his wallet. "Bet me."

"You're on." Brazen, I discard my shirt.

He leans down and sucks on one nipple, and then the other. "You're going to lose this bet."

"Well, wait. What are we betting?"

"Mystery prize," he says. "When I win, I'll think of what I want. Right now, I'm too fucking horny."

Same, bad boy, same. I prop on my elbows as he undresses, so I miss nothing. Lean muscles ripple as he tosses clothing aside, piece by piece. A wolf stares at me from his left pec, and I wrench my gaze from its silvery eyes and black fur to admire the chiseled abs and etched v leading straight to...a pierced cock.

"Whoa, what's that?" I ask about the silver barbell protruding from the head of his penis.

"Prince Albert." He glides his hand up and down the thick length. "You'll still feel it with the condom but one day I want to fuck you bare."

"I'm almost there," Lucy screams. "You're a king."

Praise be. Never thought I'd ever wish Austin would make her orgasm. Who cares if he's a king? I'm about to experience Prince Albert.

"You realize three minutes is only one-hundred eighty seconds," I taunt.

With hooded eyes, he captures my bottom lip with his teeth. "Your dirty talk is killing me," he growls.

No more dirty talk takes place because he devours my mouth, and slides the tip of his cock in, so slowly I might die before he reaches full capacity.

"Your pussy is so hot." He stills and his dick twitches inside me. "Let me show you how it's done."

And then it's on. He pumps, grinds, rams, working his piercing against my g-spot and it's all too much. Too good. Every electrified nerve tingles and when he rakes his teeth over the lip ring, the warmth building low in my belly explodes all the way to my nipples.

"Holy Sweet Tattoo Jesus," I cry out.

"Yeah, keep coming," he says. "I feel you coming."

There are no squealing yelps or exaggerated moans, just exquisite feels. All the feels as he thrusts through my orgasm until his body shudders and he releases with a gorgeous arc of his body.

"Damn, Chloe. That was..." He pants. "That was amazing. I think I broke my dick coming."

That's how I roll. Who's boring? Not this girl.

FIVE

GOAT YOGA with Charlotte is as ridiculous as I thought it would be, and thrice as smelly. Animal odors from the vast farm waft into the barn where miniature goats trounce their little hooves amongst the women snapping photos.

"This is the easiest workout I've ever attempted," Charlotte says, extending a long leg behind her, "but let's never do it again."

I laugh. "You don't enjoy having your fingers chomped on?"

Her chocolate eyes slide over to me. "By Mr. Charlotte-to-be, yes. Furry animals, no."

Heather, our laid-back instructor, leads us into a downward dog position. "Keep awareness of your center," she says. "Breathe in positivity, and release negative energy into the outer realms of the universe."

Easy for her to say, difficult for me to do. Carl, my salt and pepper sort-of friend, has taken a shine to me in a passive-aggressive way. Bounding up to nuzzle my arm before kicking me. Goat shenanigans won't deter me, because I need to release as much lingering negativity from the sex fiasco as possible. My lungs fill with air and I let it out in a long exhale.

"Focus on your third eye," Heather says. "Let your baby goat put you in a cheerful place."

As I envision myself a cyclops, Carl climbs onto my back and lovingly deposits a turd before vaulting off to nip my nose.

"Thanks, Carl," I mutter. Just like a man, it's hard to stay annoyed when he's so darn cute. That thinking will be my downfall.

"Oops. Sorry, let me get that off of you." A smiling employee, in charge of keeping the area sanitized, promptly reaches in to remove the unexpected gift and offers me a free T-shirt.

"To think, you were on the waitlist a month for that," Charlotte says. "Next time, yoga with cats."

"It's not that bad," Positive Me says.

We muddle through a few more poses, but no one here is interested in the physical and that's a good thing because concentrating is an impossible feat thanks to Carl's shrill bleat—an uncanny impression of Lucy's sex sounds.

All week, I've done my best to forget the traumatic incident by avoiding Lucy and Austin, and this is not helping. Since everyone is snapping pictures, I take one of me and Carl and send it over to Dune.

That goat looks like he wants to kill you, is his reply. A few seconds later, he sends another message. ***My brothers think they should call you Kid***.

Carl shrieks and I agree with his assessment. ***I don't want to offend the brotherhood, but no?***

He then sends me a list of better names.

Things To Call Chloe Besides Kid:

1. ***Wild Pussy***
2. ***Sweet Pussy***
3. ***My Pussy***

Nosy Carl bites my fingers as I type back, ***I like yours much better. I'll put them in my…spreadsheet.***

Mm, can't wait to see the data. Gotta ride.

"You're blushing," Charlotte says as I stash my

phone into the provided container so Carl can't eat it. "When are you seeing Dune again?"

"He's out of town at a motorcycle rally. Maybe when he gets back?"

I'll admit, I can't wait to see him again. He's like having one chip; you just can't. If he can do that in three minutes with a bad arm, I can only imagine what it will be like with two good ones. We haven't made any future plans, and I unburden my worries about Lucy's claim that we're an odd couple while a tan goat licks Charlotte's caramel skin like candy.

Carl ambles closer and shrieks an inch from my face. "Please stop. You're reminding me of Lucy."

Charlotte's head whips to me. "Lucy? Spill the tea."

Big brown baby goat eyes judge me as I move into a plank position.

"So, confession," I say as another goat wanders up to nibble Charlotte's curls. "Dune and I, ya know, kinda heard Austin and Lucy."

"That's the vaguest confession in the history of confessions," she says, resting her elbows on the mat.

Everyone in the barn is preoccupied with baby goat photo ops, so I whisper the details of what happened in my room.

Charlotte beams. "Wow. A piercing? I did good, huh?"

"You did. The attraction is powerful."

"That's not surprising. Just remember, you may need to be okay with no-strings-attached sex. And that's fine. This is your daring phase."

"Yeah. It would have been better not to have Lucy and Austin tearing down the house. It feels cheapened, somehow."

"Well, I think this is the best thing. You're getting over Austin by making certain he knows about you and Dune."

"That's not...you're reading this wrong."

"No, I'm not. I'm basically never wrong," she teases, "and I'm the person who knows you guys both best."

"You are wrong about *this*." I extricate my grandmother's locket from Carl's mouth.

"Seriously, it's a great thing you're accepting that he's with Lucy by listening in on their lovemaking."

"You are wrong that I have accepted Lucy, and you are most of all wrong that what they were doing was lovemaking, given the snatches of dirty talk I heard."

"You just said snatch. You *are* getting braver."

"Oh, I'm definitely getting braver. I did my own dirty talk."

"You're really coming out of your shell, my sweet little turtle. Wonder if they heard you?"

That possibility is mortifying. As far as I know, they don't even know Dune was in my room. "There's no way they heard my spreadsheet stuff over Lucy's screams."

"Did you just say spreadsheet?"

"He wanted me to dirty talk and I couldn't think of anything. And he's obsessed with numbers, so I went with it."

Charlotte laughs so hard her goat tumbles off her butt. "You can still make love while saying dirty cock-type things. Haven't you ever read a romance book?"

"I read biographies and history books, you know this."

"I learned everything interesting I know from romance books," she says. "Try one for ideas."

I cover Carl's innocent goat ears and make a mental note to download some romance books.

My next session with Dune has a lot to make up for, particularly in the lingerie department.

CALEB'S ORBS of fire lasered in on my bare pussy as I spread the drenched lips. "You want to taste my sweetness?"

"Not just taste. I'm gonna claim that pussy, and you're going to beg me to fuck you."

. . .

"WHY IS YOUR MOUTH HANGING OPEN?" Austin asks. "Still reading dirty books?"

I nod, finishing my paragraph. I've binged an entire MC series over the last week, and even if I'm unsure what to make of the motorcycle club lifestyle as written, I'm hooked. Dune is the epitome of the elusive men written in these pages, and it's thrilling: I've found my very own alpha. "Romance writers must live and breathe sex."

"It's a fantasy no man will ever live up to," Austin says, Swiffering the hardwoods. "Do the guys in your books ever mop or sweep?"

"No, they're busy capturing the moon for the love of their life."

He rolls his eyes. "Would you rather have the moon or a clean house?"

"Why can't I have both? That's not unreasonable."

"Again, it's a fantasy no man can live up to."

That is entirely debatable. However, no man may live up to Dune's three minutes. But it's seeming like I won't have another go. Between accounting and his biker obligations, there's been no romance time. Is he bored with me already? He seemed to love the likeness of his dick I made on my pottery wheel. That's definitely not boring.

After reading these books, I'm convinced he's

hiding something, though. No proof exists to bolster my theory, except Austin's endless insinuations about why I've not been to his place.

Alternative plan, ditch the internet advice and emulate a romance heroine. I'll need a troubled past, and I don't really have one. If I squint my eyes while I look back at my childhood, maybe my mom flitting around the globe as an archaeologist could be viewed as sad? Hm. Is that why I'm meeting men on a site that gives me rocks?

Surely, there's something traumatic hiding within me. Even though my parents divorced, it didn't affect my mental outlook on life. Should the fact Granny Mae was my surrogate while mom and dad pursued their careers bother me? It's possible I have subconscious daddy issues? Am I not broken enough and therefore my alpha male doesn't want to put me back together?

"What do you have for me today?" Austin asks, now Swiffering his way to the kitchen.

It's been hard to look him in the eyes since the fuck fiasco almost three weeks ago, but today I do, because this is a perfect opportunity to test my new theory. "A girl left by her father."

He stops in his tracks. "Come again?"

Ah-ha. He's intrigued. Yes, that's the aim.

I bite my lip the way Ava did in *Motorcycle*

Mayhem and wait a dramatic beat before answering in a low voice, "My dad wasn't around much."

"Isn't he a trucker?"

"Yes." To this day, when he's in town, I still enjoy going for a ride in his big rig, but that's not the point. The point is, Austin moves closer to my perceived brokenness. Interesting.

Do men have an innate urge to fix things like women?

He crouches in front of me. "It's only an issue if you make it one."

I recite a line from the book, "A good man will never want these jagged pieces. They'll only make him bleed out until he's dead." And wow, the force of Austin's reaction blows me to smithereens.

He cups my face in his warm hands. "Stop it, right now," he says. "Is this about Duke?"

"Dune," I correct.

"If he doesn't think you're good enough, that's his issue. Not yours." He stands. "Honestly, you can do better than—"

"Thank you." I decide to end this charade because now guilt is creeping in that I used him as an experiment. "I'm cured. I guess I just got wrapped up in my book."

The unexpected roar of a motorcycle saves me from the awkward situation I created.

"Damn, that bike is loud," Austin says. "You have a date?"

"No," I say, rushing to the door.

Against a spectacular sunset of tangerine, Dune removes his helmet as his muscular thighs straddle the machine between his legs. As I drink in how cool he is, Lucy's BMW arrives to mar the spectacle. "Lucy's here too," I call over my shoulder to Austin.

We step onto the porch and I make the introductions.

"Is your bike custom?" Lucy asks, admiring the shiny chrome and metal.

"Yeah." Dune explains the details to a rapt Lucy, and why didn't I think to ask that question? Lucy commandeers the conversation in an artful way, finding out things I should have asked and didn't.

Why I'm A Secondary Character:

1. Didn't ask his motorcycle club name or say "Genius" when he revealed Rocky Riders
2. Didn't know Dune is the club's treasurer
3. Thought they just liked to ride and never fathomed each member of his club must clock twenty thousand miles a year

It's time to take back my heroine status by again

borrowing Ava's words from *Motorcycle Mayhem*: "It must be wonderful to have a brotherhood that has your back no matter what. Riding the road, free"—I gaze at his bike with what I hope conveys yearning—"yet captive to each other by an unbreakable bond."

Dune's dark eyes zone in on me. "You get it. It's like you took my thoughts and stole them right out of my head."

I'm a plagiarist. I should tell Austin to get his cuffs and arrest me. But I can't because Dune leans in for a breathtaking smooch. It's heady, with a dash of awkward, as we're watched by Austin and Lucy. Dune rests his forehead to mine as if we're alone.

Austin clears his throat in a reminder we're not. "We'll just head inside. Don't forget to let me know what kind of cake you want."

"Chocolate," I call out as they walk away.

"Cake?" Dune asks.

"My birthday is next weekend," I say.

"Twenty-seven is a two and a seven. That's nine. The square root of nine is three."

There's nothing to say to that, so I stay silent as his eyes drift over my face. "I have to head to the club. But I needed to see you, even if it was just for a minute."

Disappointment reigns that he's busy again, but I'm going to go with it and let things happen in an organic manner. With longer days, that means when he's free, we'll have more time to spend together. Summer is the perfect time to fall in love with a bad boy.

HAPPY TO REPORT, twenty-seven feels exactly the same as twenty-six. Except for the crushing reality that I am now one year older and may add yet another failed relationship to my list. My goals are slipping further away. Silver lining—this is the first birthday of my life spent with a date. Dune has whisked me away for a surprise. Armed with the things I've learned from my romance books, I'm going to make every second count.

Wish I had read these sooner. No wonder I haven't been able to keep a man. If this were Romancelandia, I'd be worse than the secondary character. They at least get spin-offs. I'd be the co-worker, or neighbor, who only shows up when a scene needs more people. I have been Comatose Chloe all along.

"So do you ever read books?"

"Nah. No time."

I've spent the ride trying to know Dune on another level besides physical, trying to find out what makes this bad boy tick. He's powered by adrenaline, and we have nothing in common. Well. That's not totally true.

Things We Have In Common Besides Nothing:

1. We both love his tattoos.
2. See number one.
3. See number two.

The wind swirling through the Jeep takes my sigh and carries it away. "You know, twenty-six is two and six. And six divided by two is three," I reach as Dune drives us toward worlds unknown. "I've known you in two three phases of my life."

"Don't say those things unless you want to get naked."

I lean on the console, chin in hand. "It *is* my birthday, and there's that whole birthday suit thing and all."

I'm becoming a pro at seduction after reading erotica. Dating a bad boy is bringing out the bad girl in me.

"Don't tempt me. We're almost there," he says,

placing a hand on my thigh and trailing a finger toward my maidenhead. Now there's a word I never thought I'd use, but romance books use it, so there ya go.

"How much longer?" Excitement mounts as to what my birthday surprise entails. We've been cruising backcountry roads in the Jeep for close to an hour, and Dune has remained tight-lipped about where we're going. He's a man of few words, and I get it. When you look like him, you don't even need to speak. My phone rings, and I glance at the screen to see I've just answered a FaceTime call from my mom.

"Happy birthday, honey," she says. "Twenty-seven years ago, I was pushing you out of my vagina."

"Mom," I say. "I'm not alone."

"I'm sure they know how childbirth works," she says. "It's not a pretty thing. Who are you with?"

"Dune," I answer.

Dune leans in a bit. "Hi."

This is not how I thought this would go down, and I change the subject. "Where are you, Mom?"

"At your grandmother's."

Granny sticks her face to the phone. "Happy birthday, honey. When are you coming to visit? Will Dune be joining?"

She continues to attempt an interrogation,

shaking her head in the background as Mom breaks in to tell me about her new dig. Dune speeds down the road, occasionally chuckling under his breath as they squabble. Well, this is my family and this is what you get if you end up with me. We hang up with a promise from me to call as soon as I get back.

"Sorry about that. It's their tradition to harass me on my birthday."

"No worries." With a grin, he makes a fast right onto a road shadowed by dense woods. "Five minutes."

Curiosity overwhelms me as he navigates to a trailhead filled with a hodgepodge of cars. He zips into an empty space and parks.

"What is this place?"

"So, I wanted to take you somewhere special for your birthday, and Lucy had a great idea."

"Lucy?" Oh, dear. Why on earth would he ask Lucy and not Charlotte?

"Yeah, I saw her at the mall while I was looking for new boots."

"Ah."

For some reason, the disappointment is strong knowing he gets his gear at the mall. I'd like to think there is a special alpha shop that caters only to bad boys. There was in the BB Easton book. At any rate, none of that matters as he continues, "Ready for part one of your birthday surprise?"

I smile. "So ready."

"We're camping. My gift to you."

In a perfect display of my feelings, crickets chirp from the trees surrounding us. "Camping like a tent, fire, and sleeping bag? Or glamping like a cabin, electricity, and a bed?"

"The real deal, sweets. Two days of roughing it."

"Oh, wow." I'm scheduled off from work, so that's not a problem, but the last time I went camping was never. I haven't had the best luck connecting with the outdoors, but how can I say no to something I totally hate when it comes from those lips? Besides, this will be a bonding experience. Long, hot days just means more time to spend together, I remind myself.

"Sounds fun." Why in the heck would Lucy suggest camping? "I didn't bring any clothes, obviously, so..."

"Don't you worry that pretty head of yours. I have everything covered."

To thank him, and also to hide my disappointment at not being able to back out of this, I slide my hand against the pulse beating fast in his neck and press my lips to his. "This is so sweet."

"Don't tell anyone."

He exits and removes a backpack from the rear. And his vest, of course. You have to admire his dedication to bikerdom in the sweltering heat. "It's a long hike to the campsite." He wanders over to the brush in front of the Jeep and forages through the grass. "You might want this." He holds out a knobby branch, half the length of my body.

"Why would I need that?" Wary, I glance over to the narrow dirt trail leading into the woods. "Is something going to attack me?"

He chuckles. "It's a walking stick. Nothing will ever attack you when I'm around. Guarantee it."

His protective words are sexy, but... "Anywhere you're going that requires a *walking stick* is much too far."

"It will be worth it."

Hand in hand, we set off down the path. About a hundred miles into the hike, I search for a positive to counter the negative of my aching calves. It's at least ten degrees cooler beneath the thick canopy of trees, so that's good. Fewer chances of rattlesnakes. Sunlight filters through the leaves and needles, leaving a different mosaic of diamonds as we shimmy through brambles and hop over twisted tree roots for hours on our endless trek.

"What do you think so far?" Dune asks when we stop for a water break.

"It's a thicket of beauty," I say, knowing Lucy would swing by her shiny hair from the trees with a smile.

Tensions rise when Dune reveals a shocking twist.

"Yeah." He replaces the canteens in his pack. "We could've driven closer to the site, and did a five-minute walk, but I wanted you to experience this with me."

I point my stick at him. "You mean there was an easier way?"

"There's always an easier way," he says. "But what does that get you? Besides mainstream."

I could list the things it gets me, but unfortunately, I'm too tired. Then he makes me forget all about my ruffled feathers. "Two roads diverged in a wood, and I—I took the one less traveled by.

And that has made all the difference."

Goosebumps flare across my sweaty skin. "You just quoted *The Road Not Taken* by Robert Frost. Are you even a real man?" I whisper, with bones of poetry putty.

He rubs his generous package and stalks closer, eyeing me like prey. "I think you know just how real I am."

Up against the rough bark of a Ponderosa pine, with a knee-buckling kiss, he makes me forget how

I've chosen the simple path all my life. Voyeur birds trill as his tongue swoops in and flutters against mine. Much too soon, he breaks away.

"We should go," he says, dropping three quick kisses on my lips. "Don't want to stir up the animals." He rocks his hips against me. "Or do we?"

As much as I want to continue, the threat of wild animals overrules the ache between my legs. Besides, there's always a fire risk here, and this is dangerously hot. "We should probably go. Finish this at camp."

With a move straight out of a romance novel, he slips a finger beneath my shorts, into my panties and through my wetness. "I need a taste to hold me over." He sucks the wetness from his finger, and I'd hike ten more miles for a chance to have him look at me the way he is right now. Okay, maybe five. Three. Yes, three.

We continue on, and just when I'm ready to use this stick to vault out of here, he offers a reprieve. "It's up ahead."

"Thank you, Tattoo Jesus," I say as we approach a clearing.

My steps slow, wondering if I'm dehydrated and seeing a mirage ahead.

In the packed-dirt open area are four large tents, Adirondack chairs, balloons, a biker couple and...my friends. Even Lucy and Mr. Charlotte-to-be are here.

"Surprise," they yell.

I'm so tired, and shocked, tears mix with the sweat flooding my face.

"I can't believe you did this," I blubber, latching onto the vest I'm not supposed to touch. "And brought my friends."

Dune pulls me into his hard chest. "Figured you'd like it." He whispers in my ear, "Plus, wasn't it fun when we outbanged your roommate the first time?"

Everyone surrounds me and overly-hot hugs abound, so I'm able to ignore his comment.

"I can't believe you're all here," I say. I'm astounded they agreed to this since it's literally camping. Like out in the wilderness. If they also had to hike all day to get here and there's no cell service... They must truly love me.

Dune throws an arm on my shoulder and introduces me to his biker friends.

"Jackal and Angel, this is Chloe, my old lady."

The look of horror on my friends' faces can't deter my pleasure that I've reached the esteemed old lady status.

"She's youthful and in her prime," Charlotte interjects. "Quite bendy!"

"No disrespect intended," Dune says with a sheepish grin. "It means she's my woman."

"Oh," Charlotte says. "Don't mind me then."

Austin cocks a brow and I challenge it with a lift of my own.

Lucy interrupts our dueling eyebrows. "This is so fun," she says. "I love camping."

Of course she does. She probably whispered to the animals on the hike here. They probably set up her tent for her. I vow I'm going to love it too.

I'M out of my element and I do not love it. And I'm still competing with Lucy. Not to complain, but who goes hiking after a hike?

Dune points to a wooden sign with a diagram of a winding trail that's labeled in bright red letters *Advanced*. "Let's do this one."

To my surprise, Lucy says, "I don't know about this one."

"I know," I say with gusto. "I know it's going to be fucking great. Come on, pussies."

Reading those romance books really gave me a whole new level of comfort with words. If only I felt comfortable with this trail. Silver lining—I have all the technical rock terms I learned from Dune, so at least Lucy will be impressed by those, as we topple over the side of a cliff.

Charlotte, ever the practical one, asks questions about the dangers pinpointed on the map, and after hearing Dune's answers, my friends decide to stay behind and prepare for my party.

I don't blame them, because the trail is not for beginners. Just because I understand their hesitation doesn't mean I don't stare at them with longing as they walk away, willing them to change their mind.

"Let's do this, brother," Jackal says.

They fist bump and we set off.

While I'm climbing a mountain with Dune's friends, my friends are back at the camp, probably drinking canned wine and eating Cheetos. What am I even trying to prove?

Dune is sweet, though, helping me along the way. Even riding me on his back for a bit. The trail ends in a glorious wildflower meadow full of pink mountain heather. I sink my weary bones down into the aromatic field and stare at the blue sky. Puffy clouds float across at a slow pace, kissing the distant crags.

"Now I know why you thought the trail would be worth it. It's gorgeous up here." This is life, stopping to appreciate beauty.

"Yeah," he says, "it is."

He's looking at me, though, not the flowers. Whether I can handle the frenetic pace of Dune becomes a non-issue when he picks a bouquet and hands them to me. An ache settles in my chest, and every bit of struggle to get here is now worth it. Maybe there's something to picking the road less traveled, after all.

SEVEN

WHOEVER INVENTED the portable shower is my hero. So is Jackal for arriving early to set it up at Dune's request. The thought he put into that precious amenity cancels out the fact I spent the entire day hiking and can't feel my legs.

"I'm so thankful I didn't have to bathe in a stream," I say to the girls. "He really thought of everything."

"Chloe, he's ah-mazing," Lucy says as we sit by the thankfully allowed fire, sipping chilled beer. "He was so eager to do something special for you. Hope you don't mind the camping suggestion. I know you're not an outside girl, but I figured this would be a little PR for you as an active person."

Even if she makes me feel like a freakish vampire who never sees the light of day, I can't be offended by her words, because she's the reason I had fancy shampoo and conditioner. She even took care of my clothes situation while they were at the mall and picked out the Biker Bitch shirt and bedazzled jean shorts I'm wearing. I can't wait to see what features on the hoodie I'll be donning as the sun sets.

"I don't know if she needs any PR," Angel says. "She's already his old lady."

Thank you, Angel. I like her a lot.

"Speaking of old lady, I didn't realize you were so serious," Charlotte says.

"I kind of didn't either," I admit out loud. "But yay."

"I knew when Austin invited me to his place, we were serious," Lucy says with firelight flickering off her glossy hair. Even in this heat, it's smooth as glass. "A man's home is his sanctuary and once you've been there, it's real."

Her statement unsettles me and I shift in my chair. Though Dune's made it biker-official, our relationship doesn't feel real yet. For a man who structures his life with lists and spreadsheets, he lives by no other rules.

I glance over to where the guys are huddled, whittling or something. "I haven't been to his place yet."

"Why?" Lucy asks.

"It's only been..." Wow, it's been a little over a month, and I've only seen him a handful of times. "He's busy, so things are pretty spontaneous."

That makes no sense, but I don't have an answer so I just spewed out some words.

"Biker men are a different breed," Angel says. "Jackal claimed me only four days ago and my head is still spinning."

"Claimed you?" Charlotte drawls out with wonder. "Why is that hot, when it shouldn't be? It's like you're a territory."

"It's different, for sure." Angel smiles. "I don't see him that much, but when I do, nothing compares."

That appears to be the theme in the books I read. Women accepting the nomad men because they are exceptional at sex. I can relate.

"Party time," Dune announces. "Let's open your gifts."

A frenzy of activity takes place and several pretty packages appear for me to rip open under a sky filled with twinkling stars. It's perfect.

"I made you this," Dune says, handing me a carved piece of wood. "A better walking stick. I whittled in our special number."

"I love it," I say, softly. While Charlotte "aws" I stand on tiptoes to brush my lips against his and recite a line from *Motorcyle Mayhem: Book Seven,*

The Reckoning, "I only have myself to give you. It's not much, but it's worth something."

"Damn, girl. You're making me feel things."

I'm horrible, but aren't we all?

Just when I think nothing can top the moon-shaped cake Austin baked from Granny Mae's recipe, he pulls out his guitar.

"I wrote a song."

Flames flicker an orange glow as Austin rests the instrument on his lap and softly strums. His raspy voice sings about a girl rewriting history so a moment can repeat itself. The moment where she realizes she's in love. My gaze slides to Dune, who listens with narrowed eyes, and I force my lips into a smile. It's just a song. It's not like he's singing about me. Lucy sways gently to the music with eyes closed, mouthing the chorus. It can't be about anyone other than her, because she's so secure in herself. And that's why she'll always be the heroine. She and I are two different genres, so I snuggle into Dune's side, ignoring Austin's stare, pretending I don't care who it's about, ready to star in my own story.

DAY two of camping is better than day one. If I keep telling myself that, I might believe it. Today we're canoeing, because there are still muscles I apparently haven't discovered. This time in my arms. It's like rapids kind of river rafting too. Like, maybe I might die? Water rushes downstream at an alarming pace as the men ready the canoes.

"I can't believe she found you a leather swimsuit and had a birthday girl patch sewn on," Charlotte says, shaking her head. "You still look hot."

"That's because I am hot." The one-piece suit that zips up the front and rides high on my hips is tantamount to having a scorching car seat seared onto my body. I look over to where Lucy stands in a daring red bikini. "My boobs may literally catch fire. How do they wear those vests all the time and not melt?"

"It's their lifestyle," Charlotte says. "Have to respect the commitment, even during river rafting."

Maybe my suit is pleather and that's why it's so uncomfortable? The stiff material creaks when I bend over. But I'm grateful, because otherwise that would make me a petty bitch. Not today, Satan.

"Off subject, but who is Coco?" she asks.

I shrug. "I don't know. Dune had to leave the night we met because she was sick. Why?"

"This morning, I was getting coffee and overheard Jackal ask Dune how Coco was doing. When I asked Angel who Coco was, she clammed up and said it wasn't her story to tell." She nudges my shoulder. "So I thought you'd tell it."

"If I find out, I'll let you know." I'm all kinds of curious, but getting anything out of Dune is near impossible. It's like a secret society I can only access through my new favorite books.

"Ready?" Dune asks, stalking toward me in an arousing display of bare chest and vest.

Because I value my pitiful life, I hesitate until Lucy squeals and holds an oar above her head. "I've always dreamed of this," she says with a wiggle of her hips.

Austin smiles at her display, and I look away. Last night, when we retired to our tents, I crawled onto the blow-up mattress with Dune and promptly passed out from exhaustion. When I woke in the middle of the night and poked my head out of the tent to make sure the grunting I heard wasn't a wild boar, I caught an unmistakable sex shadow show on the wall of their tent. Figures, Lucy was bumping and grinding while Comatose Chloe slept in both her hoodie and also Dune's, because it's cold at night in the mountains even in summer.

"I'm ready," I say.

"Front or back?" Dune asks.

"You shouldn't say things like that unless you plan on getting naked," I taunt in a low voice, brushing past him. Romance heroines have anal all the time, and right now, I'm willing to sacrifice my virgin butt to the God of Bad Boys to get out of river rafting. With a loud squeak of leather, I crouch by the boat, and push my booty out in what I hope is an enticing way.

"You're so bad," Dune says. "Get in. I'll reward you later."

"Chloe," Austin calls out, sprinting over to us. "Wear this." He holds out a life jacket.

"She doesn't need that," Dune says. "I've got her."

"I'd feel better if she wore it," Austin says, jabbing it at me.

"I've got her," Dune says.

"You sure about that?" Austin says.

"Do I look like I'm not sure?"

While they silently communicate by staring at each other, Lucy calls out, "Come on, babe. Little sister will be okay."

"Thanks for your concern, but I'm good." I turn toward the canoe. "Let's do this."

Like a twisted version of Noah's Ark, we enter canoes two by two and drift away with the current. It's not as bad as I thought. Dune and I take the lead, moving far ahead of the pack, and it's exhilarating.

"We're going to go a little off course," Dune says

steering us left in a zigzag until we catch air paddling through frothy water churning over rocks. As I scream, it's apparent that not accepting the life vest was an unwise decision. If I go over in this heavy ass leather suit, I'll sink right to the bottom of the frigid water.

"Paddle harder," I yell, gripping my oar so tight it's fused to my hand. "Are you even fucking paddling back there? Dig, man, dig!"

"The worst part is coming up," Dune shouts. "Keep it steady and straight."

"You realize water moves, right?"

He calls out instructions and somehow, I remain focused on staying alive. It's amazing what you can do when your life is in danger.

Lucy's squeals of delight behind us are like salt in an open wound. Our canoe tosses precariously as water crashes over the side, and I wait for my life to flash before my eyes. It doesn't. Probably because I'm too boring.

Once we're past the "worst part," and the water calms to a tranquil flow, my pulse continues to race. Like might-be-having-a-heart-attack racing. Never have I experienced anything like that. Dune acts like we're on a vacation cruise and steers us over toward an embankment and behind an overhanging tree.

"That was wild," I say. "But I will never be so foolish as to refuse a life vest again."

"Told you I had you." He pulls out his dick. "Only thing better than the wild is fucking in the wild."

He strokes the hard length. "Remember I told you I'd think of what I wanted when you lost our bet?" I nod, fixated on the way he's pleasuring himself. "Blowjob. You were so sexy out there, I need to claim your mouth."

"What if someone sees?"

"Let them see."

I'm into it, actually. Turns out there's something irresistible about these daredevil sex addict types, because I twist around and crawl between his splayed thighs. "Suck me," he says.

One thing I gleaned from romance novels is to make sure I use eye contact, which is impossible while I place kisses along his cock.

"Where's your piercing?" I ask.

"Took it out for the trip."

Bummer. He moans when I flicker my tongue against the sensitive skin on the underside of the head.

"You've got a beautiful mouth," he says. "Rub my dick against it."

Pre-cum leaks from the tip as I gloss my lips.

"Mm, yeah," he pants out.

I glide his thickness down between my breasts and borrow another line from Ava. "Feel how fast my heart beats for you?" I tap it against my chest, and add a few of my own words so I'm not an outright thief. "Thump. Thump. Thump."

He sucks in a ragged breath. "I want to fuck your tits."

Now I feel silly for complaining about the zipper. It's perfect for this moment. I ease the metal down to cradle his dick in my cleavage. No one has ever titty banged me, and I'm amazed at how sensual it feels. With an instinct I didn't know I possessed, I squeeze my breasts tighter and lick the tip every time it shoots up.

"Oh God," he says, jerking faster and reaching out to pinch a nipple.

The way he moans, the way his abs contract when I take him in my mouth, causes my clit to pulsate. I want to get myself off with him, but in an unselfish move, I slip a finger to his perineum and caress the sensitive skin.

"Holy fuck. Suck me faster." His head falls back on another loud groan. "I'm going to come. You feel too good."

I suck tighter, relaxing my throat and taking him as deep as I can without gagging. It's all so daring.

Especially, how public it is, a fact that really hits home as Dune finishes and comes all over my face. I look up and see that Austin and Lucy's boat is only a couple rapids away.

How embarrassing.

Or thrilling? Austin seemed to have an impressed look in his eyes before he smirked at me self-righteously. Judge away, buddy. This is why you didn't get a near-death blowjob.

"You look so hot with my cum on your face," Dune says.

Thankfully, I can clean my face in the river. Dune is a good man and insists on fingering me until I think I might die again. This time, an exquisite death. We head back to camp, and I avoid Austin while we pack up our things.

Overall, the trip was a success. I think. Until Dune dodges my not-so-subtle hints to let me go home with him. Maybe he's not that into me after all?

JUST GOT DONE WITH WORK. **Meet me at Handle Bar**, Dune's text reads.

Since I haven't seen him this week, due to his endless biker activities after work, I should be rolling out of bed at breakneck speed. But I'm not. My body is only interested in relaxing after the camping trip. It's a whole mood.

Most important, I'm at a really good part in my novel. Ava may love another man, and the thought I might not get the ending I want is too much to bear. But the fact that a heroine would never lie in bed rather than go to her man isn't lost on me. I toss my novel aside and pad to the living room where I catch Charlotte, her fiancé, and Austin watching *Sons of Anarchy* on mute while reciting Dune lines at the TV. All three of them are crying with laughter.

"You *guys*."

Charlotte gasps. "I'm sorry. It's not fair of us."

"Not fair to Charlie Hunnam, anyway," Austin says. "Wasn't Dune on an episode of *COPS* last week?"

"Oh my God. He was not. Actually, honestly, I don't know. It does seem sort of on-brand," I admit. "Maybe he *is* hiding a gambling ring at his house."

"Or a meth lab," Austin suggests, to more of Charlotte's giggles. He needs Tattoo Jesus.

I smile too because it is kind of funny how him dodging inviting me to his place has resulted in nefarious theories from everyone. I'm feeling a bit like an old lady in name only. It's not that I want to be attached at the hip twenty four seven, but it would be nice to advance to more than weekend thrill seeking. A sleepover would be nice. But also, if I want to feel closer to my boyfriend and farther from Austin, I should probably be spending more time with the former than the latter. "I'm going to go draw some fake tattoos on with a Sharpie and then go see him."

"You wouldn't," Charlotte says.

There was a time her words were true. But the daring side I'm exploring so would. And does. In my art supplies, I find what I need to create an homage to our hike, complete with a road and flowers, on my bicep. A romantic gesture like this should definitely get me an invitation to his house.

"What do you think?" I preen for the trio and explain the meaning behind it.

They're impressed with my skills and assure me it looks real. Until Austin touches it and smears a patch of my beautiful buds.

"Oh damn. I'm sorry," he says, looking less than remorseful.

"It's fine," Charlotte says. "It looks like an early morning mist has settled on the trail."

"Yeah, that could work," I say. "It was a little hazy."

"Probably from the smoke he's blowing up your ass," Austin mutters, moving toward the kitchen.

I follow him and watch as he wipes down the already clean counter. "Why don't you like him?" I finally ask.

"Why do you?"

The gauntlet has been thrown down. My list of reasons seem a tad inadequate.

Why I Like Dune:

1. He's sexy, duh.
2. He has a pierced cock that I'm trying my best to experience again.
3. I don't know.

"He quotes poetry and gave me flowers and was nice to my grandma." Much better. I place my hands on my hips and give him a mighty hard stare. "And, most important, we have chemistry, and he likes me."

"If you have three seconds to spare, you'll have to put that in your spreadsheet," he says, turning to drop the sponge in the sink. "You'll need a new column for all of it."

Good thing he's not facing me to see my face erupt in fire. Maybe I was louder that day than I thought? He knows. And he knows I now know, judging by the smug look when he turns back around.

"Actually, I don't have any time at all. Don't wait up, *my king*. I'm off to see my prince." With that, I wink and leave. But I only make it a few steps out of the kitchen, before I peek my head back in. This man baked me a moon-shaped cake and I don't want to leave with tension in the air. "In case you were wondering, sponges were invented by accident in nineteen thirty-seven from a defective batch of foam."

He smiles. "Thank you. I was definitely wondering."

I'm feeling pretty good about my artwork and mature decision to smooth things over with Austin as I Uber to the bar to meet Dune.

When I arrive, Dune waits outside for me, leaning against his bike. Thankfully, Austin's wet-blanket attitude didn't put a damper on my attraction. Just the sight of his jeans, T-shirt, and vest causes an insane flip flop in my belly. On my approach, his eyes travel from my sandals, up my sundress, and stop on the artwork.

A lazy grin lifts his lips. "What's that?"

"You like?" I stop in front of him. "It's our path...on a misty morning."

He rubs his thumb across the path which is now dry. "You know what I'd like better?"

"What?"

"You've inspired me. I want to take you somewhere."

Surprises never bode well for me. He takes my hand and we cross the empty street.

"Something tells me if I ask where we're going, you won't tell me," I say as street lamps light our way down the sidewalk.

"That would be an accurate assessment."

He leads me a few blocks to a blue concrete building with tinted windows.

"What's this?"

"Skin Deep."

"Cool name. Care to elaborate?"

"It's an exclusive members-only tattoo shop."

"Are you going to get another tattoo?"

"You are," he says, opening the door.

I laugh. "I don't think I'm ready for a real one."

"Just check it out."

Despite my reluctance, we enter the shop. A blonde-haired man, wearing punky glasses, greets us from behind a horseshoe-shaped counter.

"Hey, man," he says. "You here for more work?"

"No, she is," Dune says. "Max, this is Chloe. It's her first time."

"This is Sharpie." I point to my arm. "And I haven't decided to get one yet."

"Pretty impressive. You drew that?"

I nod, basking in the praise as Max leads us to a room with drawings of three-eyed animals on the wall.

"You'll never forget your first time," he says.

Sometimes, things spiral out of control. Art is discussed, and you feel a kinship with a fellow artist. You decide you want to add some honeysuckles to the flowers from the meadow, because you love honeysuckles. Ten minutes later, you're seated in a tattoo chair, and you don't really know how you got there.

Max readies his equipment—all reassuringly sterile—and I close my eyes when he wheels up next to me.

"Breathe," he says. Unfortunately, I have forgotten how.

The saran-wrapped padded leather armrest of my torture chair is crushed beneath my fingertips. Chilled sweat erupts on my hot forehead as I clench my teeth with enough force to turn them to powder. His torture device connects with my skin with rapid pricks of fire.

"If there is hell on earth, this is it," I say. At least I try to. What comes out is more of a strangled groan.

The torture stops. "You okay, Chloe?" Max asks.

"It's too soon to tell."

"Give us a minute," Dune says.

Max wheels his chair away and tosses his gloves in the small hazardous waste trash can. "I'll get you some water."

When he's gone, Dune leans in and traces a finger along my cheek. "You gonna survive?"

"I've endured worse." For the record, I have not.

"Why don't you open your eyes and watch? Might make you feel better to see what's going on."

"Nah, I'm good. Thank you, though."

"Sometimes pain can be pleasurable." He licks his lips. "Intense pain can be like a sexual experience for some people."

"Maybe he isn't doing it right?"

"You want him to make you come?"

My eyes widen. "What? No."

"Relax"—his sensual voice is just the right octave to make my body react—"let it feel good."

I lower my voice to a hush, "I'm all for having a light spanking, or my hair pulled, okay? You can even choke me. A little. Gently." Like I said, I've learned a lot from romance novels. "I'm just not into pain that makes me bleed."

The only sound is the light whoosh of air through the vents above me. "God, you turn me on," he breathes out. "I want to get between your legs and eat you out, right now. While he marks your skin."

My mouth opens, but no words form.

"The honeysuckle symbolizes happiness. Did you know that?" The warmth from his hand sears my skin.

"No, I didn't know that. I picked it because I like to lick the little bead of dew from the tip of the stem."

His eyes drop to my mouth and his tongue peeks out to wet his lips. "Lick, huh? You don't suck it off?" A flush creeps across my face. "Why are you blushing?"

I tuck a strand of hair behind my ear. "Max might hear you."

"And? You're my woman, and I don't care if another man hears."

"Well, you said that thing..." I hesitate. This is

not what I expected when I made the rash decision to come here tonight. This is way out of my comfort zone, but for some reason I'm not making any real effort to leave.

"What thing?"

"You asked if I wanted him to make me come. Which, I have no idea how you thought that was going to happen."

"Oh, he could," he says, slipping a hand inside my sundress to palm my breast. "For some people, a tattoo is erotic. The sting of the needle is like a bite to the nipple. Or a slow lick to your clit and then a nip with teeth." His eyes sweep over the exposed skin of my thighs. "Every pass of the needle over the skin is sensual, like nails digging and scraping into your back during a hard fuck." I stare at his mouth, mesmerized by the low husky tone of his voice. "Your body heats. Your heart races. It builds in intensity until you feel as if you're going to come. You fucking want it. You need it."

I clench my thighs together. What is going on? I need to get out of here before I shove his head between my legs. Or...I could do it. One leg, then the other over his shoulders, my heels pressing into his back, his face buried between my thighs.

"You ready to finish?" Max asks, just as Dune removes his hand.

"We'll see." I take a chug from the bottled water he offers me. "Maybe I'll faint and won't even feel the rest."

Dune's phone buzzes. "Fuck, I have to take this," he says, brushing past Max and out of the room.

"Maybe I should come back another time?" I look down at the artwork on my reddened skin.

Max sits, using his inked-up legs and Converse-clad feet to roll up next to me. "I've barely touched you yet."

"I really don't want to do this anymore," I whisper. "I think I just want to go home."

He slides a hand along his scruffy jaw. "Look, you've got an inch line."

"That can mean something, right? Like, a reminder to not cross a line."

We both stare at my arm as if it's suddenly going to blossom.

His teeth rake along his bottom lip, with a piercing much like Dune's, then stop. "Why did you want this?"

I sigh. "Dune..."

"Stop right there." He leans back in his chair. "You never mark your body for anyone else."

"I wasn't marking my body for him." I was marking it about him. Ugh.

He narrows his eyes, studying me. "I don't believe you. But I believe you know better now."

I tilt my head at him. "You're a wise man."

He spreads some ointment on my line and covers it, giving me instructions how to care for it. I move to get up as Dune returns.

"I've decided I'm not ready. Thank you, Max."

"Any time."

I tip him for his thwarted work, then we head outside and although I don't want to mark my body for him, I do want to finish what Dune started while we were alone.

"Something has come up," he says, thwarting my plan of going to his place before I can even voice it. "I'll walk you back and take you home."

"Is everything okay?"

He runs a hand through his hair, leaving it in disarray. "Yeah."

Since this isn't the first time he's put me off, as we rush back to his motorcycle, I have to wonder... *is* he Breaking Bad?

NINE

GRANNY MAE IS RIGHT—PERSEVERANCE
pays off. Just when you think something will never
happen, it does.

"Want to come over to my place?" Dune's text
reads.

My fingers squeal with glee as they type, "I'd love
to. What time?"

"An hour?"

"Perfect. Have something to share with you. See
you soon."

Ah, we've reached the milestone of sharing
things. For lack of a better comparison, this would be
the part of a novel where meaningful things happen.
What did I do to level up? Possibly that trick with my
tongue on his perineum. Thank you for that bit of
wisdom, romance writing gods. He sends me his

address and I shower and shave all my bits, and dress in record time.

"I'm going to Dune's house," I announce with satisfaction to Austin and Lucy.

Lucy gasps and bounds from the couch. "Let me smell you."

I tuck my chin to my neck as she rushes toward me in a blur of tanned limbs. "Why? I showered."

"Excuse us," she says over her shoulder to Austin, taking me by the elbow with a firm grasp and leading me to the kitchen.

"I'm going to share a secret with you," she whispers, releasing me at the counter. "But it's between us, okay?"

"Okay."

"I've never shared this with anyone. But I feel I'd be derelict in my duties as Austin's significant other if I didn't share this with you."

They're not married, so I'm not sure a significant other is an appropriate moniker. But that's neither here nor there. "Well, my curiosity is piqued."

And stays piqued, because instead of telling me, she chews her pink glossed lip while fingering the strand of pearls around her swan-like neck, studying me. "After the camping trip, I'm invested in you two making it, so..." she trails off.

"You're really fantastic at the suspense building," I say. "Please, tell me."

"You want your scent in his house. You want it everywhere, Chloe. All over, in every nook and cranny. All the most frequented places in his home."

"Why?"

"It's a subconscious mind trick." She leans against the counter, speaking in a hushed tone, "He won't be able to stop thinking of you. Guaranteed. It's like magic, but not black magic. In biker terms, you're marking your territory."

Ah. Lucy uses trickery. Simple, yet brilliant. "I didn't know this."

"I did a campaign with a new company and learned pheromones are the secret to attraction. Just a few drops in your perfume is all it takes to imprint yourself."

Honestly, and I can't tell her this, I'm not sure I want to imprint myself, just yet. I know from the Twilight movies that imprinting is permanent, and I still have a lot to learn about Dune. Even my tattoo artist sees that. "I'm more of a lotion girl. I'm sure I exude my own pheromones?"

She leans in and sniffs me. "You smell like soap."

"Is that bad?"

"Men are most attracted to floral scents," she says. "And vanilla is always an excellent choice.

Hold, please." She reaches in her Prada bag and produces a square bottle of perfume. "Dab this behind your ears, on your neck and wrists. And then find places to lay your scent. His pillow, couch, anywhere you can."

I do as I am told, because while I'm uncertain whether Dune is my lifelong mate, it doesn't hurt to dabble in trickery to ensure he stays around long enough to find out. "Thank you," I say. "It's really nice of you to share your secret with me."

I'm extra nice because I feel extra horrible for wanting to immediately disinfect the house to rid it of her scent. If she is a romance heroine, I've got to try not to become the villain. And that's an even better reason to mark Dune's house, so I once and for all get rid of this Austin thing.

"I've got to say... I'm still so surprised by you and him. He's not who I thought you'd end up with, at all."

Something tells me not to ask her to expand on that, but I do, "Who do you picture me with?"

"Well, it's hard because you don't really go out. But I can see you with an accountant, just not a biker accountant. But again, Boring Belinda really shocked me, too." Her words have no time to offend me when she pulls me in for a tight hug. "I feel like we've really bonded." She releases me. "I'm glad we get along so well. I haven't really done the whole bonding thing with females. Ya know? My therapist thinks it's an abandonment issue because my mom went on a sabbatical to France for a few years when I was seven."

Fascinating. Lucy has a tragic past. I knew I needed one.

"And what do you think about that theory?"

"I think I've just been busy building my career. I want to be president by the time I'm thirty-five."

She really is goals. Women like her deserve to be the heroine.

"What are you two doing?" Austin asks.

"Just girl talk," Lucy says, smiling, and semi-breaking girl code. "Wanted to give Chloe some pointers on how to make this permanent with Dune."

Austin's eyes slide to me as he passes on his way to the fridge. "She's a smart girl. I think she knows this isn't permanent. Unlike the line on her arm."

Touché. Lucy rolls her eyes, but of course, it's in a cute way. If I did it, I'd just look like the bitchy secondary character.

"Well, thanks for the vote of confidence, Mr. Sunshine. I have to get going or I'll be late."

While Austin's head ducks in the refrigerator, Lucy rubs herself against the counter in what I'm guessing is a reminder for me to mark Dune's home. I smile and give her a thumbs-up before Austin turns around and hurry outside so I'm not late.

As I approach my car, Austin calls out to me, "Chloe, wait up." He jogs over to me and holds out a small spray bottle. "Take this."

"Do I really smell this bad?"

"It's pepper spray."

"Austin—"

"Just take it," he cuts in. "I'd feel better knowing you have something to protect yourself."

"You don't have to worry about me. I'm an adult," I remind him.

"I'm very aware of that," he says in a low voice.

Awkward settles in, because I shouldn't be wishing he meant that in a non-brotherly way.

"Thank you," I say, turning away from his penetrating stare to escape.

His arm shoots past me, brushing against my breast in the process of opening the door. Wild horses gallop through my chest. And they shouldn't. He steps away as if I electrocuted him and I bolt into the car to hide my disgraceful hardened nipples. "Okay, see you later."

When will this crush ever abate? I drive away without checking the rearview mirror. My future lies ahead, not with the guy standing in the driveway.

And ideally, it's where the GPS leads me, and not to jail when I start smuggling arms for an MC.

WHY CAN no one ever tell me things in advance?

The directions on my phone lead me straight to...the gates of Pres's house?

"How can I help you?" a man's voice asks.

"Tell people to stop surprising me?" I answer and then laugh to play it off because this is a biker gang. "Dune, please."

The skull-emblazoned gates swing open, and I follow the drive to the front of the house where Dune's bike sits parked amongst a row of several other Harleys. I park, grab my purse, and roll with it. Sigh. When I step onto the porch, I get a weird vibe that someone is watching me. My eyes slide to the right and I *am* being watched. But not by someone. By some*thing*.

I stop mid-step. A hairy white creature, with owl-sized blue eyes, sits on its haunches staring at me. Tiny bottom teeth protrude from the exaggerated frown on its face.

"Help," I whisper. Whatever the thing is, it looks enraged by my presence.

For minutes our gazes lock, mine stunned, its judgy, until it rises and takes a step toward me.

"No! No!" I shriek and reach for my pepper spray.

In a flash, Dune appears in the doorway. But instead of shrieking too, he scoops it up...and cuddles it? "Did Chwoe scare you, widdle fwuffer-muffin?"

My heart rails against my chest. "Is that your pet?"

He strokes the long white mats in its fur. "This is Coco. She's a cutie, huh?"

This is mean, but you know how every proud parent thinks their baby is the most beautiful even though half of them just look like red, wrinkly old people, but you could never say that, so you lie? That's what I do. "So cute. Is she a...cat?"

Coco's exaggerated frown, grumpier than Grumpy Cat's, does not approve of my question.

"Yeah." He twirls one of her dreadlocks fondly. "This is why I haven't had you over yet. Come in."

He steps aside and I enter the tiled entryway, feeling Coco's unending stare on my back.

"I thought we were meeting at your place."

"This is my place."

"Excuse me? Isn't this Mr. President's house?"

He scrubs a hand along his jaw. "Pres is my dad." He holds up a finger when my mouth drops open. "I just needed to make sure we were solid before I told you. Someday I'll replace him and things have to stay close to the vest. Get me?"

"Um, not really. You live here?"

"For now. Until I win my house back."

"Win your house back?" I parrot, because this is a lot to digest.

"Yeah, lost it in a race to Jackal last week." He shakes his head. "Fucking crazy. But I always honor my debts and next week, I'm going to get it back." He's confident, so that's good.

"Why didn't you want me to know you had...a cat?" My brain cannot come to terms with the fact that I am more surprised that Coco is a cat than the fact Dune wagered his house away.

"I don't like to introduce her to people I don't think will stick around." He looks at me from beneath those thick lashes and utters the one sentence that can erase all the wild things he said prior. "It's important to show your babies stability, you know?"

He said *babies*. The effect on my body from that word is tenfold compared to looking at his tattoos. An ovary explodes when a vision appears of leather-vested cherubs rushing to meet Dune at the door after a long day of biking. Gah. Another of Dune rocking a chubby version of himself in a Harley onesie has me surreptitiously rubbing myself against the wall of his temporary home so he'll think of me coming and going. The other ovary remains intact, riddled with resentment, because it knows I've been home tending to our cherubs, a tired, hot mess, while he's out seeking thrills.

"I've never had a pet." And certainly not one with saucer-sized eyes that don't blink.

"It's a big responsibility," he says. "Like having a kid."

"Do you want kids?" spews from my mouth before I have a chance to close it.

He strides into the living room and picks up a plush fish toy from the hardwoods. "It's on my list. Number three hundred."

I perch on the arm of the sofa and rub my wrist along the back, marking it. "What's the number before it?"

"Swim with sharks."

My wrist marking halts. "Wasn't expecting that."

He ranks swimming with sharks above having children. Why is that troubling? I should be thankful he's not someone who is ready to rush into anything, but—

I can't complete that self-analysis, because he says, "Would you do it with me?"

"I'm guessing you mean swim with sharks and not sex?"

His eyes dart to Coco. "Yeah, uh, we can't have s-e-x with the baby around."

It's cute he spelled out the word, if not a bit strange.

"Do you have a bathroom?" I need a private moment to process my feelings, which naturally means I need to text Charlotte. After he directs me to the hallway bathroom, I snap a covert pic of him with Coco and type out a message to Charlotte.

I can't decide if this is the most hilarious or the sweetest thing ever????

SWEET GOD. That isn't real! Did he hack that up? Was he grooming the beards of his motorcycle gang?

Charlotte is not helping. But I can't blame her. It's a lot to wrap your brain around. Especially when we move to the kitchen for a dinner of burgers and fries and I discover that Coco has her own seat at the table.

While Dune baby talks to her and she stares at me with unabashed hatred, I take another picture. I might be a little annoyed Charlotte couldn't talk me down, but goddamn will we have fun making memes out of this later.

TEN

DATING DUNE IS GOOD, mostly. It's been a couple of months, and I don't get to see him as often as I'd like. Translation—never. It's summer, so he's got lots of biking trips, and that's cool, right? Gives me time with my friends and my art. And it's nice to say I have a boyfriend but not have the time commitment. Or the Coco commitment, which is the one giving me cold feet.

When he's in town...well, that's pretty good too. We're getting more comfortable with each other in the bedroom. And by that, I mean I've sat on the bed and had numerous stare-offs with Coco while he showered. It's all good. Except something is missing. In particular, his house. Jackal disappeared on "business" so Dune hasn't been able to get it back. I'm currently living the plot of a romance novel. I know it's my summer to be daring, but I'm not wired to keep up this pace.

Andrea, my favorite and also only co-worker at It's Clay Time, had given me an idea for something I'd been searching for ahead of Charlotte's wedding.

It's an out of print book, a tongue-in-cheek retro guide to marriage, that I want to get Charlotte for a bridal shower gift, but it's nowhere to be found. *Something Borrowed* is a pop-up that I'd completely forgotten about, but they are currently popped up in a bookshop I can easily walk to on my break. With any luck, I can manage it before my allotted fifteen minutes with Dune this afternoon between his club meeting and his club ride.

The morning class passes in a blur of ceramics, and after I tidy up and prepare to leave for my break, I walk out from the back to find Dune standing by the counter. It's earlier than I'd expected. I am now distracted.

"Hi," I say. "Already done with your club meeting?"

He turns to me, and good God in heaven, my pussy doesn't stand a chance. He didn't shave. The scruff that covers his jaw is begging to scrape my thighs.

"Hey there." His husky voice grates against my nipples and a seismic tremor of guilt passes through my stomach when he says, "Had to drop Coco off for some behavior therapy. She's regressed and keeps marking her territory all over Dad's house. But I've got a few extra minutes now, if you don't mind me joining your lunch break."

Unfortunately, Lucy's pheromone trick worked a little too well. Coco is now at war with me. I cringe and silently ask for forgiveness.

"You're probably the one who will mind," I tell him, linking arms and setting off down the road. "I've got a wedding book to find." He just smiles like none of it matters.

A chime tinkles when we enter the store that's hosting, and a petite woman with gray hair asks, "How can I help you?"

"Hi. I'm searching for an out of print book called *I'm Not A Bad Wife, You Are.* I heard the *Something Borrowed* rack might help?"

"Let me check. Sounds familiar." She moves to a freaking rolodex, because bookstores live in the last century, apparently, and rifles away. "Yes, I have it."

"That's incredible." I beam. "I can't believe I found it. This might be the only one in existence."

"Just follow the stacks all the way to the back. Shelf twelve. Alphabetical order. I'm Mildred. Let me know if you need further help."

Dune trails behind me as my giddy feet carry me

to the rear of the store. I scan the packed shelves and —bingo.

"It's your lucky day," Dune says.

"Shhh. Lower your voice," I tease, pointing to a vintage sign that reads, "Whisper as if you're in a library."

His teeth capture his full bottom lip and then release it.

"Let's see how quiet you can be." He presses against my body and I grip the edge of the shelf. "You shushed me, like a naughty librarian. What a fucking turn-on." All the hair twisted on top of my head, held prisoner by a thin black band, tumbles free with a tug of his hand. "I want to wrap your hair around my cock. Slide the silkiness up and down until I come."

"Um, I don't think we can do that here."

He trails a finger up my quivering thigh, taking my skirt with it.

"Red lace," he says, looking down at my panties. "So wicked."

"Dune," I whisper. "What are you doing?"

Apparently getting on his knees and spreading my legs apart.

"I'm going to eat lunch."

Oh my. Fear of getting caught battles with desire when he glides a finger along the edge of my panties and pushes them aside to dip his tongue inside. One long, slow lick up to my clit.

Mmm.

I mean, "We can't do this here."

He buries his face, sucking the bundle of nerves while I grind my hips and peek through the shelves to make sure no one is coming.

"You're so fucking wet." He inserts two fingers.

The smell of antique books and Dune are a powerful aphrodisiac. Almost as powerful as the orgasm that buckles my knees when he pumps his fingers and laps his tongue against my clit. He picks up a stamp sitting on a cart and presses it to the top of my pussy. "Marked as mine." He rises. "That was all the time I had. I have to get going. I'll call you later."

I'm so breathless, I can only nod as he stalks away. He stamped my vagina. Like I have an actual date in ink. I reach down and lightly skim my fingertips across the area he marked. How sexy he marked me. And how wrong for me to think it's sexy. I shimmy my skirt down and walk from between the shelves of books on rubber legs. And come face-to-face with Mildred. She looks particularly snappy with her pinched lips and stiff back.

"Found it. Woo-hoo."

She crosses her thin arms and glares. "We can't help you," she bites out.

My eyes widen. "Excuse me?"

"This store is meant for reading, not sexual cavorting with the town bad boy." Her frosty tone leaves no room for negotiation.

"I really need this book," I plead. "I'm so sorry. I just..." Once again, let my libido overrule my head. "He's got tattoos," I whisper.

"Do you think that impresses me?"

I meet her icy stare and clutch the book in my hand. "I...I would like for you to give me another chance. It won't happen again."

She shakes her head and turns away.

In desperation, I quote a line from *Motorcycle Mayhem*, "You don't understand what it's like to be with a man like him. He's a nomad, and I'll never be able to hold on to him. So I'm greedy and take all I can when he gives it, because one day I know he'll be gone. And I'll have to survive on these memories."

She halts and pivots on her loafer. "Did you just quote *Motorcycle Mayhem*?"

I crumple into a leather club chair. "Yes. I'm a sham."

"Brilliant series. Read them all twice. I've learned a lot from those books."

"Yeah, well, romance books may have helped me gain the man, but what now? Nowhere did they mention what to do to keep the man. The epilogue was s-e-x. Pfft. I need to know how they're still together five years later, ya know? Where's *that* book?"

"No one would read that." She chuckles and then turns serious, "I had a man like him once, and besides that"—her eyes point to our clandestine corner—"what's he doing to keep you?" She takes a seat opposite me. "That's what they don't write about. The mundane things, the stuff that makes them your best friend."

Like mopping a floor while you read a book.

"I don't think he's very mundane."

"Well, you just need to introduce it and see if he can handle it."

"That's a good idea. I'll test the waters." Hopefully, they aren't shark-infested. "What happened to your guy?"

"Left him when he accidentally set my hair on fire. I should've stuck with his friend. But we all have our one that got away, I guess."

Wow, Mildred lived a triangle.

"I enjoy being alone, though," she says, and man, that's depressing, because the wistful look in her eyes says otherwise.

She rises. "Let's ring up your book."

SPEAKING OF A BUCKET AND A MOP, it is really fortunate that Dune likes pussies so much.

Tonight, the hellcat is at a sleepover, and Pres is out doing presidential things, so our mundane night in is now a marathon to make up for him being gone. It's going well—after oral satisfaction, my reverse cowgirl giddy-upped into doggy style. No offense, Coco. He drives his steel shaft into me at a frenzied pace, pushing me to the precipice of orgasm with his piercing. *Shaft* is another word I've underutilized until reading romance. In my head, it's always *penis*, *dick*, or *cock* if I'm feeling spicy. Now there's a plethora of words to keep it interesting.

A whole new column, so to speak.

Penis Words Besides Penis:

1. Love Rod
2. Pork Sword
3. Mushroom Headed Fuck Stick

As my orgasm crests, Dune pulls out.

"You ready to take it up another notch?"

"Another notch, and I'll be on the moon."

"I've been holding back until I felt you were comfortable." With his condom-sheathed love rod leading the way, he walks over to the closet and returns with a large black box. "I think you're ready."

"That sounds ominous."

He opens the lid and no, I'm not ready for what I see lying on the velvet interior. A whip and a variety of sex products, some with metal pointy things, fill the box.

"Well, this is unexpected," I say. And really, why is it? His need to have sex in the open was a big warning sign that Here There Be Kink.

"Don't worry. I won't hurt you too bad. Pick a safe word."

Why is life so hard? Can't a girl just get an orgasm?

"Succotash," is the first word that comes to mind, and I have no idea why. A line forms between his brows. And now I feel I blew my safe word choice. "No, wait...hm...pie chart."

His cock bobs with approval. "Damn, it'll be hard to stop, but I will. Let's pick what you want to try."

This is way beyond my wildest imagination, but I can do this. It's like a game of trust, in a way. Not to toot my own horn, but it's amazing how I can rationalize doing things I don't want to do. There must be some kind of award for that? I deserve two of them.

"This gadget gives a shock to your nipples."

"Oh, dear. What else do you have?" I'm not a bad girlfriend, you are.

He removes a roll of what appears to be duct tape. "This won't stick to your skin."

"Next." I shake my head in disapproval as he goes through the products and God help me, I circle back and pick the nipple zapper. And it's every bit as bad as I thought it would be. He moans at my discomfort and teases the tingling peak with his tongue.

"Pie chart," I say when he zings my other nipple.

"Really?" he says.

I nod, and he drops it but things spiral further out of control when he kneels and pulls straps from beneath the bed. "Let's try something different."

He lies flat on his back. "Restrain me."

Oh, okay. This I can do. In a few minutes, I have his hands and feet restrained. His erection points at the ceiling and I ease myself onto his thick length. He groans as I move up and down, letting his piercing work its magic. Until...

"Choke me," he says.

"I don't know that position."

"Put your hands on my throat and choke me."

"Like stop you from breathing?"

"Yeah. When I get ready to come, it'll be a hundred times more intense."

The future flashes, and it ends with a horribly embarrassing obituary where he dies from auto-erotic asphyxiation and me explaining to our biker babies that mommy accidentally choked daddy to death. No way can I come with that thought in mind, and my tiny hands can barely make it around his neck.

"Count to sixty before you let go," he says, after I continue letting go after only ten seconds. "Numbers are your friend, remember."

Somehow he manages to finish and say nice things even though I know I failed at actually blocking his airways.

"We'll work on it, babe," he says.

I thought I was a liberal woman. But this is a problem. Because as much as I want things to work, I'm not sure if I'm into making this my lifestyle.

ELEVEN

I WAS today years old when I learned they make motorcycle helmets for cats.

"This is going to be so f-u-c-k-i-n-g cool," Dune says, holding a helmeted Coco in his arms.

Why is it so adorable he's spelling out the curse words? And why does a man so gentle with his cat want to electrocute my nipples? There has to be a happy medium, and I'm determined to find it.

"Ready to make some p-u-s-s-y pottery?" In what I think is a brilliant attempt to bond and introduce Dune to something I enjoy, I offered to make a clay likeness of Coco. Maybe my motives weren't so pure, because I'll do anything to avoid having kinky sex again. I'm still wildly attracted to him, even after the choke fiasco, but now it's overshadowed by my fear of pain. Since I finished my romance series, and they are living happily ever after in their crime-riddled lives, I've reverted back to the internet for advice.

An interesting article on dating a bad boy pointed out that I'm probably most attracted to Dune's sense of adventure and rebelliousness, hence why I keep coming back for more. Seems reasonable. Personally, I think it's the tattoos, but alas, I'm not the internet expert. A reasonable adult would say the straightforward thing would be to tell him about my hesitation, and I pledge to do that, eventually. Right now, I'm content with avoiding it, because that's what I do. I'm running out of excuses, though.

Reasons To Not Have S-E-X:

1. Pulled a muscle in my vagina getting off his bike
2. Migraine, possibly from the nipple zapping
3. Nauseous

That last one wasn't a lie, actually. I ate an entire box of Ho-Hos trying to come up with excuses not to have s-e-x. Another thing the article pointed out was that in order to have a functional long-term relation-ship, we need a deeper connection. Obviously, I knew this, but when you're overcome with lust, you kind of forget how to think. So I need to detox from the physical and get my head together.

Making pottery will be good for us as a couple. Except, Coco is particularly frowny today and I really need her to get over her dislike of me and cooperate. Her round blue eyes watch me with disdain as I set up the wheel.

"Pottery can get a little messy," I explain on his dad's patio, since he still hasn't won his own house back.

"I like messy," he says, stroking Coco's Muppet-fur. Sunlight glints off his lip ring, and I do my best not to let it mesmerize me.

"First, you take this ball and throw it." I demonstrate the clay throwing and well, Dune does not seem interested until I spin the wheel and use my hands to work the clay into a shape.

"S-h-i-t," he spells, "looks like you're working my d-i-c-k."

A heavy weight of disappointment settles on my chest that this, too, is sexual, but I kind of forget that when he says, "Daddy is going to try it now."

Visions of our leather-vested babies toddle into my mind. "You're really sweet when you say that to Coco."

His husky voice causes the fine hairs on my neck to stand on end when he says, "I wasn't talking to Coco."

My hands slip along the wet clay as I stare at him. "I don't understand?"

"I was talking to you. Haven't you ever called a man daddy?"

"Yes. My dad," I answer, feeling like my bonding tutorial is spinning out of control faster than the pottery wheel.

"Tonight when you c-h-o-k-e me, I want you to call me that."

My clay collapses. "I really don't think I can do that," I say. "See that line on my arm, I kind of can't cross that one."

"We'll try it," he says. "Life is about pushing boundaries."

"I'm just not sure I can call you that while we're f-u-c-k-i-n-g."

"Why? It's like saying I'm the man who takes care of you."

Pres's deep voice interrupts our conversation, "Dune, impromptu meeting. Need to go over some numbers with you."

"Sorry," Dune says, "I have to go." He places Coco on the ground and I swear she hisses when he walks over to me. "Meet me this evening. I'm racing to get my house back. I'll text you where to go."

That sentence alone should have me rethinking my sanity. He wagered his home away, and I'm still fixated on the way his dark hair flops over his eye, like it too refuses to be tamed.

Dune brushes his lips against mine before scooping up Coco. "Mommy will have to finish you another day."

Coco's eyes grow from saucers to plates, nearly touching her tiny helmet. I'm sure mine are as large, because I'm not ready to be a stepmother. My brilliant idea to bond no longer seems brilliant. Instead of romance novels, I should download self-help books. Dune disappears inside, but his dad lingers as I clean up my mess and start packing the portable wheel. Bet Dune never called *him* Daddy, or he would see how weird it is.

"You're a nice girl, Chloe. His cat seems to like you."

I wipe my hands on a towel. "I thought she hated me."

"Nah. She'd claw your eyes out if she did."

Well, that's disturbing. I make a mental note to purchase goggles. "Listen, my boy can be reckless, but he loves hard." Why is that appealing? "It takes a strong woman to love men like us. His mother wasn't. Make sure you are."

I nod and he leaves me standing in confusion. The pressure is overwhelming as I drive away, because I have no idea if I'm strong enough to love myself, much less Dune.

"WHY DO YOU LOOK SO GLUM?" Charlotte asks as we lounge on a grassy hill near a construction site, waiting for Dune's race to start.

After today's events, I needed moral support and Charlotte's presence calms me. If you'd told me at the start of this relationship that two months later I'd be watching my boyfriend stand by a Harley with his biker friends preparing to win back his house while I'm dressed in a leather catsuit gifted to me by Lucy for my birthday, I would have probably laughed. And then did it anyway, because I make horrible decisions.

"I had a terrifying vision that I choked Dune to death." I've not been able to shake the sense of dread of having to "work on it."

"Chloe"—Charlotte's brows pull together in a unibrow—"do you have those kinds of visions often?"

"Oh my gosh, no," I exclaim. "I'm kind of appalled you think I'm a secret psychopath."

I explain the kinky sex situation. And everything after.

"Whoa," is her response. "You've gone far beyond daring. You may need to back up, turn around, and drive back to start."

I pluck a blade of grass and run it through my fingers. "Why can't he just quote poetry and make love to me in a meadow?"

"What are you going to do?"

"I don't know. I need to tell him, but I don't want to shame his kink."

"There's a chance he'll take it off the menu."

I shake my head, wishing it were so. "I swear I saw cans of unopened red paint in his dad's garage. Oh God." My head whips to her. "He's planning to make a Red Room, isn't he? Charlotte, I am not that pain tolerant."

"I gathered that from the one-inch tattoo."

Why didn't *he* gather that? You need a magnifying glass to see my attempt at ink. What part of "I don't like pain" did he not understand?

"Of course, at times, he will probably want me administering the pain, not receiving it, which somehow feels even more daunting. I read some think-pieces on dungeon mistresses as research. I think I might"—it's hard to admit, after all this work —"I might not be a bad girl."

Charlotte, as I already knew she would, literally falls over laughing.

I swat at her arm. "Stop it. If *I* fall over, it will ruin my Sandy-from-*Grease* vibe."

That just sends her into more hysterics. "That explains the getup." She hums "Goodbye To Sandra Dee," before segueing into an INXS song. It takes a second, but then I can't help it, I'm laughing too. Though I personally feel the vintage-Domme look suits me.

"All jokes aside," she says, composing herself, "are you still into him? Like butterflies in your stomach?"

"Yes," I admit. "But...we're only having sex. I've tried, and I can't seem to tip us over into something more. And even if I could, I don't have the backstory to be a dominatrix. Even if I'm dressed like one right now."

I've spent ample time online reading up on the BDSM lifestyle and I know in my heart it's something he won't give up. And I don't want to end up with my hair on fire like Mildred. It's not Lucy's hair, but I do like it.

"Can I be honest with you?"

Her dark eyes meet mine. "Aren't you always?"

"For the most part," I say, watching Dune and his friends huddle around their bikes. "I really want to fall in love with Dune. He's so hot. And he's...hot. That vest, and the bike, and the tattoos. It's a lethal combination."

"Ugh, I know," she says. "But Chloe, how much is the attraction based on the bad boy appeal? I'm not judging, because I picked him for you based on that, but from a psychological perspective, the good girl wants the bad boy based on the hope she can change him."

"I know I can't change him." I sigh. "Those romance books really made me want this to work. But can it?"

"Well, they're an escape from reality."

"That's pretty much what Austin said. He said they cause unreal expectations because they say everything a real man wouldn't."

"Just because *he* doesn't say them doesn't mean other men won't."

"That's part of the appeal, I guess. Finding a man who makes you feel like you're his entire world."

"Do you really want to be someone's entire world? That's a lot of pressure."

"Well, not to the point that I can't breathe. *Don't you dare* make a choking joke. But someone who would never lie or hurt me? Or dump me when something better comes along? Sure, I'd like that."

"Those are givens, Chloe."

I'd like to believe that's true. But so far, I haven't experienced it. Dune hops on his bike and rumbles up the hill over to us.

"Chloe, I need a kiss for luck."

"Swoon," Charlotte whispers.

"I'll be right back," I say.

Dune is sitting sexy on his bike when I make it over to him, stacking mental bricks on my wall with every creaky leather step.

"Damn, you look hot," he says, wrapping an arm around my waist. "I can't wait to have your hands around my throat while you're wearing this."

Ugh. I was hoping he'd say something like "I can't wait to get my house back and show you around." But I am prepared. Even his tattoos aren't making a dent in the armor I've erected.

"Is that something you must have?"

"Yeah," he says, matter-of-fact. "You'll like it once you get the hang of it."

This choking thing is a hard limit for me.

I can't believe I'm about to say this... I think I need to break up with him before I accidentally murder him. But I can't use my fear of auto-erotic asphyxiation as the reason. "This is bad timing, I know, but..."

He revs his engine, drowning out my words.

"Hello, um, could you not do that? I have something important to tell you. I think..."

The faint sound of sirens wailing interrupts me.

"Fuck," Jackal shouts. "Cops."

"Oh my God," Charlotte says, popping up from her seated position. It's easy to do in jeans.

Dune revs again when the sirens get louder.

"Get on," he says.

"No, I can't."

"I can outrun the cops, don't worry. You won't get arrested."

"Well, I can't leave Charlotte."

"Get on, Chloe. There's always a casualty."

Leaving a friend behind is my hardest limit of all, so I stop procrastinating. "Dune," I say. "I have always admired you." He smiles, but looks back at the flashing lights approaching and pats his seat again. "I think you have a novel approach to...everything. And numbers... well, I did not know numbers could be so fun."

"Numbers *are* fun, right? I can go from zero to sixty in three. Here, you'll really want to be wearing a helmet for that part."

"AnywayyouarereallysuperbraveandI-

likethataboutyoubutitsfranklytoobraveformeI-
thinkweshouldseeotherpeoplehereisyourhelmetIamsorry!"
I throw out as fast as I can so it's over, and also so he
can race off.

He does, and as he zooms away, I hear his voice
faintly on the wind, "Remember me at tax time!
Refer   three   friends   and   receive   a
discoooouuuuunnt..."

And then he is gone.

TWELVE

THE FOURTH of July is an explosive holiday. And I don't mean the fireworks. I may literally explode from envy seeing Lucy in the kitchen in her underwear while Austin makes her breakfast. Well, not underwear exactly, some kind of yoga shorts that show her SuperButt cheeks. Something I would never dare to wear, even though this is my summer of daring. I sigh, because I failed at that too.

Of course they are happy while I'm single yet again. Why am I faulty? Is it my diet? Lucy is going to enjoy egg whites with kale, prepared by a barefoot tousled-hair god who is enraptured with her, while I pull a frozen cheesecake out of the freezer.

"What are you doing tonight for the Fourth?" Lucy asks, taking a seat at the breakfast table.

"I'll probably pull out the pottery wheel or read a

book." All I need are tiny violins to finish off how pathetic that sounds.

"No Dune?" she asks. "It's a holiday."

"And I would think this is his favorite holiday," Austin says, dropping a chunk of butter into the skillet. "I picture him lighting a firecracker in his mouth for thrills."

My cheesecake lands on the counter with a thunk, and I remove a knife from the block. "I'm afraid we won't be seeing him until tax season."

Austin takes the knife from me and runs it under hot water. "Did he go to jail?"

"No. Nothing like that." Turns out the police were going somewhere else than the race site.

On the drive home, I felt I needed to give him a further explanation for my breakup, so I sent him a text explaining my reservations about his kink and my accidental homicide vision. Charlotte agreed that was the mature thing to do, even if she was still smarting that he was willing to sacrifice her to get away. As if. Hoes before bros, always.

Anywho, long story short, Dune said he'd miss me, but he understood and if I ever wanted a booty call, he was down. As long as he was in town and Coco wasn't home.

I slice a generous piece of cheesecake from the foil tin, place it on a saucer and take the rest over to the table. See, I'm a good person. I didn't take the whole thing. So why can't I have nice things?

"What's he doing? Out of town?" Lucy prods.

I take a seat. "We broke up."

"Oh," she says with wide eyes. "I'm so sorry."

"I'm not," Austin says, separating eggs with one hand. Show-off. "I'm glad he's gone."

"I'm not," Lucy says. "He was fun."

Now I feel worse. Lucy would've tied him up with her hair, choked him, and called him Daddy with no qualms.

"I think Chloe thinks craft fairs are more fun than jumping into a volcano. And I would agree. I'm not going to say I'm sad to see this end, because it seemed his break-all-the-rules mentality only applied to her rules and not his."

The way he says it gives me an inappropriate little flutter as I shovel in cheesecake and watch him cook. Was Austin jealous of my relationship with Dune? Score. Maybe he's planning to give me the "he was all wrong for you" talk again. I can't imagine anything more romantic in my depressed state. But thankfully, I don't have to chastise myself for that shameful thought, because he says, "Now we can stop keeping all our best jokes about him to ourselves."

"Austin," Lucy says, with a slightly cringe-y face. "Maybe it's too soon?"

"Wait, what?" I glance between them. "There's more jokes?"

"Oh, man," Austin says, sliding a perfect omelette onto Lucy's plate, "you do not know how hard it's been to hold back."

"That was you holding back?" I deadpan, remembering all the times he did not hold back.

He nods. "Want us to cheer you up and show you what you've been missing?"

They're an "us" and I'm not anymore. "Sure."

Lucy and Austin do an impression, clearly oft-practiced, of what they think Dune must be like in bed.

"Oh yeah, count the number of pumps I do!"

"One pump...two pump..." Lucy is... Is she imitating the Count from *Sesame Street*?

"Threeeeeee pumps, now slap me around! Harder!"

Oh, *dear*. That hits a bit too close to home. Utterly horrified, I rise from the table, nearly knocking over my chair, and flee the kitchen, cheese-cake in tow.

"Chloe," Austin says, "come on. Don't go."

I turn around and re-enter the kitchen. "I'll have you know, I broke up with him only for the sake of my future children. And out of respect to them, I don't think you should make fun of him."

The fact that Dune conjured up babies is really something I didn't expect.

"Aw," Lucy says, with sympathy in her eyes. "We were just trying to make you feel better. That's what friends do when you have a breakup. You need to think you're not to blame, even if you are."

"I appreciate that," I say, unsure if I do. "I've never broken up with anyone before. So I'm fragile right now and wondering if I made a mistake."

"You didn't," Austin says.

Deep down, I know he's right.

"Why *did* you break up with him?" Lucy asks.

Knowing they use cuffs, and who knows what else, I can't bring myself to spill the specifics about Dune's sexual proclivities and the Daddy thing, so I condense the truth into the short version.

"Because he thrives on adrenaline and I thrive on..." I sag against the counter. "I don't know what I thrive on but I know it's not that. I'm lucky to be alive. And even if I could change his behavior, I don't want to. I don't want to stifle him. He needs to be free and live his best biker life."

"Ah. He was a freckling," Lucy says, digging into her breakfast.

"What's that?" I settle back in my chair.

"A summer fling," she says. "It's when you have a summer romance, but you realize they're not who you want to spend your life with. It usually fades, like freckles from the sun, when autumn rolls around."

"I love that," I say. Autumn would have been three months. Although, I ended it on the third of July, which is fitting.

"Who knows, maybe he'll re-emerge next summer, like freckles."

"Oh God," Austin says, with a roll of his eyes. "Can't we just let him ride off into the sunset and let Chloe focus on her business? Must we already resurrect him?"

He slides a plate in front of me with a beautiful crescent-moon-shaped omelette. "You're too good to me," I say.

And he really is. I don't deserve this omelette. If he only knew how many times I wished Lucy to be a freckling. To thank him, I clean the kitchen after we're finished eating and make sure everything is neatly arranged in the dishwasher, as he likes it. It's a nice distraction and gives me time to find the positives over the last few months.

Instead of berating myself for the missteps, I'm proud of myself for ending it. If Dune can tell me he needs the kink, it's a step in the right direction that I realize my needs are just as important. I can only bend so much before I'm permanently curved. I'm not a prude, but I saw some wild things in my search for knowledge and I'm just not ready. Say yes to nipple-zapping one day and the next you're sporting a bushy tail and indulging in pony play.

But if not for Dune, I wouldn't know anything about spreadsheets or found a new love for romance novels or stepped out of my comfort zone and found my limits, so I can't say I regret him or our freckling.

I'm kind of sad to lose his friends, though. And his piercing. Oh, well.

Austin and Lucy get ready to leave to spend the rest of the holiday at her place. Before they go, Austin finds me in the laundry room, organizing my art supplies while I wait for a load of clothes to finish washing.

"You want to come with us?" he asks.

"No. I don't mind being alone." Oh God, I sound like Mildred. But I really don't mind it.

He rests his T-shirt clad shoulder against the doorjamb. "I know I gave you a hard time, but it's because I think he should've made more time for you."

His words are sweet, but they hurt because...I don't want to think about why they hurt. "Bikers are a different breed, I guess."

"You're a different breed, Chloe. He didn't realize it, and I knew he didn't realize it."

Man, the feels. I turn my back to him so he can't see my face, because I'm sure it will give me away, even if my words don't. "Did you know that early sea voyagers washed their clothes by putting them in a bag and tossing them overboard to drag behind their ships?"

He chuckles. "I didn't know this. But again, that's what I'm talking about."

I don't tell him that just like Finn, I never shared history facts with Dune. That might make it seem like it's our thing, and Austin and I really shouldn't have a thing. "Well, breakups suck. No doubt about that. But at least I was daring this summer."

"Yeah," he says. "Now you need to be daring in your artistic life and get Mae'd With Love going. The Fall Thing is coming up and you've got a stockpile growing of things to sell."

"We'll see," I say. "I'm not sure what's holding me back from my goal, other than fear of rejection."

"Your stuff is good, Chloe. It won't be rejected."

"I'll think about it."

"I'm going to head out. You sure you don't want to come along? We can stay here—"

"No, seriously, I'm fine." I turn to face him. "I'm not going to cry or wallow in self-pity. Maybe a little.

I don't know. I'm sad that it didn't work out, but I'm surprisingly okay. I'm just going to reflect."

He studies me and then nods. "There's some pizza in the fridge I made at the restaurant. And I saved extra marinara for dipping, like you like."

I smile. Why must he be so perfect? "Yum."

He smiles and then leaves with his girlfriend. A girlfriend who hugs me and whispers that she admires me for knowing what I want. Ugh, I suck. After cleaning the house top-to-bottom, in my ass-covering pajamas, I pour a generous amount of wine, turn on some music, grab my laptop, and move to the back porch. Fire season isn't bad this year, so for once I'll be able to catch a glimpse of neighborhood fire-works. Alone.

It's okay, because it's Independence Day. Ha.

From my seat on the back porch steps, colorful fireworks light up the sky and shower down until it burns out and fades to nothing but wispy smoke. Sort of like Dune and me. Breaking up with him might be the bravest thing I've ever done. And honestly, it might suck more to be the one who deals the death blow to a relationship. Normally, I'd stick around forever, but I'm growing and learning that time is ticking away. It stops for no one. Least of all me.

Lucy's words about focusing on her career waft into my brain. It's time I do something else brave for myself. I open my laptop and navigate to the craft fair site. The vendor tab beckons me to click on it and after five minutes I do. After draining the rest of my wine, I open the application and eeek, sign up for the Fall Thing. It's a fairly simple process, and after submitting my credit card, it's done. As long as I'm approved, I will officially have a booth. "Good job, Chloe," I tell myself, because, well, I'm single again and that's what you do when you're alone.

It's fine. Autumn will be my season.

All about me.

The Fall of Chloe.

Hopefully the in-love kind.

Chloe's dating adventures continue in *Fall Hard:*

Fall is boyfriend-sweater weather, and Ryan is exactly who I want to cuddle up with.

As the leaves start to turn, so does my luck when I get accepted to sell my pottery at my favorite art fair. And then it turns again - and again! - when my booth is double-booked.

Luckily, Ryan's good at sharing. In fact, he's quite the giver.

Did I mention he has a perfect beard?

We could easily be the cutest new couple in Boulder... if we ever leave his place.

Get Fall Hard

PAIGE PRESS

Paige Press isn't just Laurelin Paige anymore...

Laurelin Paige has expanded her publishing company to bring readers even more hot romances.

Sign up for our newsletter to get the latest news about our releases and receive a free book from one of our amazing authors:

Stella Gray

CD Reiss

Jenna Scott

Raven Jayne

JD Hawkins

Poppy Dunne

Visit my website for a more detailed reading order.

Dating Season

Spring Fling | Summer Rebound | Fall Hard

Winter Bloom | Spring Fever | Summer Lov'n

Also written with Kayti McGee under the name Laurelin McGee

Miss Match | Love Struck | MisTaken | Holiday for Hire

The Dirty Universe

Dirty Filthy Rich Boys - READ FREE

Dirty Duet (Donovan Kincaid)

Dirty Filthy Rich Men | Dirty Filthy Rich Love

Dirty Games Duet (Weston King)

Dirty Sexy Player| Dirty Sexy Games

Dirty Sweet Duet (Dylan Locke)

Sweet Liar | Sweet Fate

(Nate Sinclair) Dirty Filthy Fix (a spinoff novella)

Dirty Wild Trilogy (Cade Warren)

Wild Rebel | Wild War | Wild Heart

Man in Charge Duet

Man in Charge

Man in Love

Man for Me (a spinoff novella)

The Fixed Universe

Fixed Series (Hudson & Alayna)

Fixed on You | Found in You | Forever with You | Hudson | Fixed Forever

Found Duet (Gwen & JC) Free Me | Find Me

(Chandler & Genevieve) Chandler (a spinoff novella)

(Norma & Boyd) Falling Under You (a spinoff novella)

(Nate & Trish) Dirty Filthy Fix (a spinoff novella)

Slay Series (Celia & Edward)

Rivalry | Ruin | Revenge | Rising

(Gwen & JC) The Open Door (a spinoff novella)

(Camilla & Hendrix) Slash (a spinoff novella)

First and Last

First Touch | Last Kiss

Hollywood Standalones

One More Time

Close

Sex Symbol

Star Struck

Written with Sierra Simone

Porn Star | Hot Cop

ABOUT LAURELIN PAIGE

With millions of books sold, Laurelin Paige is the NY Times, Wall Street Journal, and USA Today Bestselling Author of the Fixed Trilogy. She's a sucker for a good romance and gets giddy anytime there's kissing, much to the embarrassment of her three daughters. Her husband doesn't seem to complain, however. When she isn't reading or writing sexy stories, she's probably singing, watching shows like Killing Eve, Letterkenny, and Discovery of Witches, or dreaming of Michael Fassbender. She's also a proud member of Mensa International though she doesn't do anything with the organization except use it as material for her bio.

www.laurelinpaige.com
laurelinpaigeauthor@gmail.com

ABOUT KAYTI MCGEE

Kayti McGee is livin' deliciously in beautiful Kansas City, Missouri. Go Royals!

She also writes as the latter half of Laurelin McGee. Like her co-author Laurelin Paige, she joined Mensa for no other reason than to make their bios more interesting. Sometimes they podcast as IRL.

Stalk away at:
www.kaytimcgee.com
KaytiMcGee@gmail.com